FISH GATHER TO LISTEN

A
HORROR
ANTHOLOGY

EDITED BY
JES MCCUTCHEN
VICTORIA MOORE
& H.V. PATTERSON

Horns and Rattles Press
Tulsa OK

Horns & Rattles
PRESS

Horns and Rattles Press

2306 E Admiral Blvd

Tulsa OK 74110

Anthology Copyright 2023 Jes McCutchen, Victoria Moore, & H.V. Patterson

Individual copyrights retained by each contributor

All rights reserved

Cover Illustration | Dustin Charles Cleveland

Interior Design | Racheal Daodu

Library of Congress Control Number | 2023913829

ISBN | 979-8-9887761-0-9 (paperback)

ISBN | 979-8-9887761-1-6 (epub)

HornsAndRattlesPress.com

@HornsAndRattlesPress

To everyone who trusted us with their stories.

Dear Readers,

When we talked about putting together our first anthology, the water called to us, and we were helpless to resist its siren song. We came from water, and all life on this jewel of a planet we call home relies on water. But water can stagnate and flood. It can carry diseases. Water destroys homes and lives. Water drowns. Human fascination with water is double-edged: fear and reverence, love and hate. We long to swim, suspended in cooling currents, yet if we swim too deep or for too long, we risk death.

Though landlocked, Oklahoma has over eleven hundred miles of shoreline, more than the Gulf and Atlantic coasts combined. Lakes carved from the ground, rivers diverted and often nearly dried to mud and quicksand. There is a decommissioned WW2 submarine that was towed up rivers and, during floods several years ago, floated again.

We might not have oceans, but we have waters. And there are obviously things lurking in them.

In this anthology, we've gathered twenty-three stories by twenty-four talented authors about the creatures, real and imagined, lurking within the oceans, swamps, ponds, rivers, and other unexpected places. These stories range from melancholic to humorous to terrifying–sometimes all three. We want everyone to enjoy this collection, so we've included trigger warnings compiled by collaboration between the authors and editors at the back of the anthology.

This is *Horns and Rattles Press's* first publication. We were thrilled and deeply grateful for the support from the horror community and the Tulsa/Oklahoma community. We love the deeply weird, the strange, the uncanny, and we can't wait to share this collection and all these amazing stories with you!

Dive in, if you dare: the fish have gathered to listen.

Victoria, Jes, and H.V.

Contents

Without Eyes, He Stares	1	Ryan C. Bradley
A Fish-Eaten Grin	3	Gabrielle Bleu
THE REAL GENUINE HONEST-TO-GOD MERMAID	15	Morgan MacVaugh
BOAT	25	Heath Mensher
psychopompós	33	Samantha Ryan
A Night Aboard the *Andua*	47	Michael Conrad
Sea People	59	Katherine Traylor
Our Yellowed Bones	65	C. C. Rayne
Singing Sweetly Through Your Veins	73	Tiffany Michelle Brown
Starfish	83	Billie Karras
Topside, Topside, Do You Read Me?	91	Amy E. Casey
From Stagnant Waters	95	Kathryn Reilly
Endling	107	Samir Sirk Morató
From The River The Penny Dropped	115	KT Wagner
The Blood We Carry	119	Annemarie Bennett
Pastorale	129	Cormack Baldwin and EV Smith
Sealskins, Daughters, Teeth	147	Malda Marlys

Daughter of the Sea	153	Hope Elizabeth Kidd
Itself	167	Jan M. Flynn
Naiad	181	Victoria Nations
Cirrata	185	K. F. Hartless
Everything You Dump Here Ends Up in the Ocean	199	Anemone Moss
There is Something Sleeping in the Mariana Trench; It Dreams of You	211	Bridget D. Brave

Trigger Warnings 219

The Authors 221

The Editors 229

Acknowledgements 231

Without Eyes, He Stares
by Ryan C. Bradley

I sit in a chair and close my eyes. The seat is straight-backed, to keep me awake. First, I focus on my breathing, feeling the air come in and go out. That occupies half my mind, and I need to picture something else to keep the rage and anxiety from rushing in. So I think of an empty beach with perfect, white sand and clear, blue water. The sun is bright, but not so much that it crisps my skin. I don't need to fight anyone to stake out a spot.

Then I watch the tide. Waves crest and then sink back down, gently splashing. Once I'm keyed in, I picture the things that are eating at me, floating out to sea. My car loan bobs a few times, and then the tide carries it out. The mortgage, all of the fights, the kids' orthodontist's bills, it all follows, until I'm unburdened.

But then, he appears.

First, his head bobs up, far in the distance. His cheeks slough off. The sockets where his eyes should be are empty. The water should pull him under. The current should drown him in the deep with the rest of my anxieties, but he gets closer.

A millipede crawls out of one empty eye socket. His red smoking jacket is smeared with blood and mud. Seaweed sits on his shoulder. Where the jacket splits, a wound reveals the white of his ribs. His stench drifts over the ocean, though I haven't imagined any smells.

I can't run. This is a fantasy, my fantasy, but my feet are rooted as the waves bring him closer. Or maybe he's cutting through them. Either way, he speeds toward me. The millipede explores the hole where his nose used to be. The remnants of his skin cling to his ribs. Water drips off him. Without eyes, he stares.

Does he remember? The argument. The knife. All over our business and a few measly bucks. But it's a stupid thought. Why else would he be here?

Finally, he steps out of the ocean, onto the sand, facing me. The stench of rot and sea salt overpowers me. The molded meat that was once a brain peaks through the empty eye sockets. Bits of skin, bile, and whatever else is left of him drip, darkening the sand. The remnants of muscles lift the bones of his left hand and point it at my chest.

The exercise ends. I'm in my straight-backed chair, more tired than when I began. I hope one day that he can forgive me. I won't rest until then.

A Fish-Eaten Grin
by Gabrielle Bleu

A drumming reverberated across the Gulf, rolling over the waves to where Raelynn stood at the console of Jacob's fishing boat. Raelynn thought it must be the engine of another boat as it struggled in the waves. There were three other fishing vessels nearby, but none were in obvious distress or emanating strange sounds. Raelynn closed in on the oil rig that was their spot for the day. Nothing in the area, boat or rig or fish, should have made that sound.

"Jacob?" Raelynn called to her cousin. He was still setting up his tackle. Meticulous and organized in no other aspects of his life except for his fishing gear.

"Yeah, what's up? Don't tell me you're tired of driving already?"

"Do you hear that?" Raelynn kept her eyes locked on the rig in the distance and hoped the sound wasn't coming from it. But as she asked the question, the sound faded, replaced by the noises of the water, the boat, and the calls of seabirds. All normal.

"I don't hear anything," Jacob said. "Are you having one of your attacks? Do you need me to steer? I'd rather turn around now than after we're all settled in and fishing."

The drumming hadn't been the sound of blood pounding in her temples during a fit of vertigo. Raelynn knew her body, and she wasn't about to faint or puke. Whatever the sound had been, it was gone, but she didn't like to take risks out on the water.

"I'm fine. Maybe let's switch, though, just to be safe."

She settled into the bow seating and readied her own gear as Jacob steered them into position beneath the white legs of the oil rig. She threaded a shrimp onto her hook, the mechanical and practiced movement a comfort to her.

This specific rig was Jacob's favorite place to fish. Rising out of the Gulf of Mexico, the structure's legs provided habitat for marine life, an alien colony site that local sea creatures took advantage of. It normally made for excellent fishing, a spot where they'd be sure to catch something soon after arriving. But today the waters were strangely empty. After a few hours and multiple checks, both of them found their bait unbitten. Their three fishing neighbors also had terrible luck, from what Raelynn could see. One of the boats, a flashy, blue 22-footer, soon gave up and moved away from the rig. The remaining two vessels looked older, their paint duller, probably owned by the kind of fisher who'd stick it out in hopes of a change in luck.

"Bad day," Raelynn mumbled.

"Maybe, let's stay a bit longer though," Jacob answered. He'd always stay a "bit longer" on biteless days, a martyr to sunk cost.

At last, beneath the slim shadow of the rig and its metal limbs, Jacob whooped.

"Aw yeah, what did I tell you?" Something was on the end of his line.

Raelynn grimaced. Jacob would be insufferable unless she landed a catch and caught up to him. Raelynn reeled in her line to check that the bait hadn't been stolen without her noticing. Half the shrimp was gone.

"Hey, Raelynn, get a look at this."

Raelynn looked away from her bait and over at her cousin. A stupid grin was plastered across his face as he held up a red snapper which looked to be a little over 25 inches. Pink-red scales gleamed as water dripped off them. Jacob held the snapper's mouth open, and from inside a pair of eyes looked out at Raelynn. White and circular, a body briefly pushed itself to the front of the fish's mouth before withdrawing again.

Raelynn had been eleven years old the first time her uncle had ever allowed her on the boat. That day, Jacob had also bagged the first catch. He'd told her he had a "surprise" before he thrust the fish close to her face.

"Want a kiss?" he'd asked, with a shit-eating grin. The fish's tongue had been eaten away by a tongue-eating louse, just the tip of its bone-white head and the black specks of its eyes peering from between the fish's lips.

She had screamed at the sight of the parasitic isopod. She remembered how hot her face felt the rest of the day, after she'd finished crying. Her uncle, not used to handling external emotions, rubbed the back of his neck and awkwardly said that "it was just a thing that happened, no use crying about it" before leaving her to herself.

For weeks she'd been upset because she couldn't explain to him that it wasn't the fish that made her cry. He wouldn't have understood her crying in embarrassment at having screamed over her cousin's prank, anyway. She'd been mad at Jacob for weeks, but he'd thought the whole thing was the funniest joke he'd ever played. He pulled the same "joke" every time they went fishing and pulled in a catch only to find its tongue replaced with an isopod. The most life the prank had seen had been the last time her uncle went out with them. He'd caught a snapper with two of the isopods crammed in its mouth, and Jacob had snatched the fish out of his hands to try and scare Raelynn.

"The fish starves when there's that many," her uncle had explained as she'd smacked Jacob away. His voice was almost mournful, the most emotion she'd ever heard from the man.

Now, it was just her and Jacob, and the joke was old, and had never even been funny. Sadly, Jacob got the boat in the end. Raelynn still loved fishing and hadn't want to give up easy access to the one connection she had to her uncle and that singular bit of emotion he'd offered to her.

Raelynn rolled her eyes at Jacob and turned away, casting back out. It wasn't worth taking the bait and telling Jacob to get stuffed. The isopods were just a thing that happened, after all, something to look for in any caught snapper or croaker, fish Raelynn still hoped to catch a few of today. She ignored her cousin's ongoing chuckles and focused on fishing.

They fished a while longer, but their lines remained slack and their bait untaken.

"You win some, you lose some, I guess. We can go somewhere else next weekend," Jacob said, packing up. He steered again, taking over the position at the console as they left behind the two remaining boats, their fishing parties even more stubborn than Jacob.

As the rig grew small on the horizon behind them, Raelynn heard it again.

Over the sound of the engine and the slapping of the waves against the side of the boat, the drumming sound returned, a croaking purr that swelled over the water. At first Raelynn thought Jacob had been right, that it was one of her fits of vertigo, that the drumming noise was blood rushing to her head. She reached out to grab the side of the boat to steady herself, and kept her eyes locked on the rig behind them as a fixed point. The wave of nausea never came, even though the sound continued. Sure that she was fine, and that the sound wasn't internal, Raelynn risked a glance overboard.

Along the side of the boat swam around two dozen Atlantic croakers, their silver, shimmering faces slipping in and out of the water as they made the drumming noise. Raelynn had never heard them croak this loudly before. She'd never seen them nose against a boat like this, either.

"Jacob," she called "come and look at this."

Jacob brought the boat to a stop and left the leaning post. The fish kept up as the boat slowed and did not disperse when it came to a stop. Jacob came up next to Raelynn to look over the side. He whistled, surprised.

"Never seen drum do that before." The fish continued to nose and heave against the boat. The cousins stood transfixed for a moment by the strange behavior of the croakers and their swelling drone. A real wave of nausea rose up in Raelynn's stomach at the continued sound, and she felt the tang of bile in the back of her throat. This panic was different than the kind that came with her vertigo attacks. Cold sweat prickled at her neck and the small of her back. She wanted to get away from the fish. Jacob seemed unaffected.

"Wait," he yelled, and rushed back to his gear. "Wait, wait. I've got a great idea." He grabbed his net, sending some of his tackle clattering to the deck in his excitement. He came back to Raelynn, dipped the net into the water, and scooped up four of the thrumming fish.

"Nice!" He held up the net triumphantly. The fins of the caught croaker glinted gold in the sunlight. A wide grin spread across his sunburned face. Raelynn couldn't match his smile. She was still trying to choke back the feeling in her throat. The fish, for their part, continued to contract their muscles against their swim bladders, the croaking louder now that Jacob held them aloft and out of the water.

"Throw them back," Raelynn said, unnerved by the sound and her body's response to it.

Jacob laughed. "No way! Easiest catch I've ever made." He paused and looked over the side at the croakers. Even more had come, a whole school of them now. The water churned with their silver bodies as they continued to bump against the side of the boat. Flashes of coral-red shone between silver as a handful of snapper joined in, unable to sing but pushing their bodies against the boat just the same. Drum were small fish, but with their numbers, the boat pitched more than it should. Raelynn had to look away as her vision narrowed to a small tunnel with only the croakers at the end of it.

"Weird, sure, but you're just mad you haven't caught anything all day. Once again, I am the fishing champion."

Jacob turned from Raelynn to get his catch into the fish box. As he did, the croakers in the water aligned their glimmering bodies and rammed the ship in a teeming, silver wave. The boat shuddered only slightly, but with Raelynn's dizziness, and her descending tunnel vision, it was enough to send her pitching over the side of the boat.

"Raelynn!" She heard Jacob yell and thought she felt his hands brush against her legs as he tried to grab her.

The Gulf swallowed Raelynn up. She twisted as she fell, trying to catch the side of the boat, and went in back first, spine curved. The impact knocked all the air out of her lungs. She was buffeted by a mass of silver bodies, enveloped in the blue of the Gulf. Fins pressed against her skin, gills brushed against her airless chest, and in the water all around her: the sound and motion of the croaking fish.

A croaker mouth pressed against hers, and something wet and writhing passed between her and the fish. The purred reverberations stopped. She thought water had filled her mouth, before realizing, after a sharp, stinging pain at the back of her tongue, that it was blood, the taste of iron instead of salt.

An arm broke through the swarmed fish and grabbed her, hauling her above the water. Her lungs filled with air. She spit up water; she spit up salt; she spit up red blood.

"Raelynn!"

Jacob shouted her name over and over as he pulled her into the boat. Raelynn fell to the hard deck as he struggled to get her over the edge. Jacob slapped her on the back as she coughed and sputtered. Blood poured from her mouth. Pain radiated from where she'd been bitten, deep in her mouth. Raelynn stuck her fingers behind her teeth to try and clear whatever was there, but it wriggled out of her reach. Her fingers started to cramp up. It became difficult to bend them, to keep trying to pull the invader from her mouth, even as the pain at the base of her tongue made her face go numb.

"Okay, okay, just stay here. You're going to be alright, I'm going to get you back to shore, to a hospital. A hospital, yeah?" Jacob left her to rush back to the center console. The croakers Jacob had netted earlier flopped and drummed on the deck where he'd dropped them, one still tangled in the net's interior.

A single drum spasmed all the way to the side of the boat. With a massive effort, it threw itself over and splashed back into the Gulf. The noise masked the sound of Raelynn's severed tongue falling out of her mouth and landing on the deck. The legs of a louse tickled her gums, and its head brushed against the roof of her mouth as it settled in, attaching itself to the leftover stump of muscle.

Her cramped fingers unfurled and closed around the severed organ which lay on the deck. It was slick with her own blood and saliva. Repulsed, unsure why she had reached out, Raelynn tried to drop her own tongue, but couldn't.

Raelynn wanted to scream, to tell Jacob what was happening, to cough out the creature in her mouth. But the isopod's influence went beyond the root of her tongue. Just like her fingers refused to work like she wanted them to, the rest of her body stiffened against her will. The tongue-eater had dug in deep, not into just one ruined muscle, but into all of them. She couldn't form words, couldn't make a sound. A wave of nausea spread through her, the sick, unsteady feeling extending throughout her whole body.

She stood up, even though she wanted to stay on the deck of the boat where it was safe. But her limbs wouldn't listen to her. Instead, she threw the tongue overboard, a reward gobbled up by the starved drum and the isopods that drove them.

The isopod that drove her thrashed about in her mouth, as it made itself a simulacrum of a tongue, helping her to form the sounds it wanted.

"Hey Jacob," she heard herself croak, in a voice and enunciation that was not entirely her own, "get a look at this."

As he turned to her, she opened her mouth wide, wide enough that he could see what was inside. The isopod, its exoskeleton the color of bone, its legs scrabbling against the soft give of Raelynn's palate. Its eyes like pinpricks peeked out at Jacob.

Jacob froze, his mouth slack. His still-attached tongue tried unsuccessfully to form words, as Raelynn's body advanced on him.

Her arms pushed Jacob overboard, into the drumming sea and the waiting mouths below. He found his voice at last, just before he hit the water, his scream cut short.

Jacob sank and did not resurface. The water churned with the bodies of croaker, of snapper, their mouths gaping open and eyes peering out from within. Hungry mouths, filled with even more hungry mouths.

Raelynn's legs and arms continued to move without her telling them to. She couldn't even focus her eyes on one solitary spot, because the isopod looked through her by using frantic jerks of her eyes. But she caught the shape of the oil rig in the distance in those dizzying glances. Another wave of nausea hit her, and she hoped that at least her vertigo would help her dislodge the creature, if she could only vomit. But unbidden signals to her muscles made her swallow down hard on even her simplest immune response.

The tongue-eating louse steered her to guide her cousin's boat back. The white frame of the oil rig rose like a skeletal giant above the blue waters. As Raelynn and her pilot drew closer to the two fishing boats that still doggedly tried for a catch, the isopod compelled her jaws to move once more. Its carapace bucked and rolled against her mouth as it helped her to form words.

"Help me," she called, at once a real plea and a trap. Her face was hot, tears on her cheeks, her tear ducts and her mind all that was left to her. The tongue-eater made her call again, and the boats began to move toward her, her voice a lure on the waves.

THE REAL GENUINE HONEST-TO-GOD MERMAID

by Morgan MacVaugh

The Boss

I dredge her up outta the stretch a sea between Atlantic and Ocean City, offa New Jersey's coastline. That mighta been the problem.

It's me and The Strongman and Gator Boy, just fishin and drinkin as the sky turns bloody with sunset. We haven't caught shit all day, cause the waves are wild and strong with weather, and we're loud with liquor. The rowboat rocks, and Gator Boy turns a deeper shade a green. We're about to row in, when there's a hard thump at the helm that shakes the whole boat. I toss the net in quicker than sin. That's how we get her.

I say 'her.' God only knows.

She's a heavy sunovabitch, so me and Gator Boy hold onto the net as The Strongman rows us in. The surf kicks up around us, and she won't stop fightin'. Gator Boy blows chunks over the other side and wipes his mouth with a shaky hand.

The sun's bled out by the time the hull scrapes into the sand. I scrabble out and pull up the net. The boys fall in behind me, and we heave. The ocean sucks in a deep breath, chokes on a shadowy shape, and spits her out:

A real genuine honest-to-god mermaid.

The Strongman

I tell him to throw it back. Sometimes there's a reason God buried critters beneath miles and miles of seawater and foam. This thing isn't meant to see daylight, to remind others of darkness.

Yet here it is, writhing and thrashing in the net on the wet sand. Making a fuss like you wouldn't believe. I can't make sense of the shape. Only that it's thinner than me. Longer than me. Slimy and mottled like a cusk fish. Spines all up its back and a tail like leather. Its face—God its *face*—nothing but mouth. A mouth full of needles.

It opens, and a hiss escapes. It's so high-pitched, it's hardly a sound.

Throw it back, I beg The Boss. The tide's coming in fierce, and Gator Boy's got this look on his face like he might yak again.

But The Boss is bent down as near as he dares. His eyes are wild, watching, and I know, God help us, we're bringing it back.

Bring the boat further in, he tells Gator Boy, *and dip it so it's full of seawater.*

The Boss stands, points at me. *Keep her netted and put her in.*

God forgive me.

Is this how he 'found' The Living Doll? Boxed up The Contortionist? Persuaded The Twins? Had all of them put up a fight save from me?

I was eight when I crushed my momma's songbird in between my fingers. It was an accident. I didn't know how strong I was, then. The bird didn't even peck at me or try to escape. I thought I was being gentle. Ever since then, I try.

I didn't need any convincing. What momma called a curse, The Boss called a gift, and I felt salvation.

God help me.

The net burns my fingers as the creature twists. A spine slices into my calf. A wicked, webbed hand reaches for the fabric of my shirt. It's still screaming. Sailors, long ago, said these kinda creatures sang. They must've lied.

I try to lay it as gentle as I can into the watery boat. The moment its skin touches water, it grows still. I fear I've killed it. I imagine another tiny heart going still against my palm.

I can't help it. I reach down to feel the skin of it, and a thousand needled teeth sink into my arm.

The Contortionist

The Boss brings back from the ocean a truth so ugly it hurts to look at.

I would know. It doesn't matter which way I look at it, no angle makes it easier. I wake all pretzeled up some mornings, like my subconscious is looking at my dreams from a new perspective. It leaves me feeling all tangled. Like I don't know who I am.

The Boss wakes the lot of us from our hammocks: the sword-swallowers, the fire-eaters, the clowns, and the acts. We all gather, and I stand and watch him watch our faces as The Strongman heaves a small rowboat into the clearing. He's sickly-looking and sweaty in the light of Gator Boy's lantern. He no sooner sets the boat down then he's trudging away, clutching his arm.

The water's black in the rowboat. The lantern casts little phantoms across its shiny surface. I see night skies and comets in it. The shape of the name my mother gave me.

Then the water starts churning, and something like a great, black fish tosses itself over in a jagged net. A pair of milk-white eyes regard the crowd and disappear under the weight of a gaping maw.

Cut her loose, The Boss says, but nobody moves.

It seems a year passes between us, until The Living Doll walks out of the ranks like a ghost. Everything about her is small, and she's so white she's almost see-through. She walks slowly up to the boat and stares into the spinning water. Gingerly, ever so gingerly, she takes ahold of the net. The creature turns once in displeasure, and settles. The Boss hands her a pocket knife and she saws at the strands.

Deep into the process, a webbed paw slips from the surface of the water and touches her face. I can't bring myself any closer.

No matter which way I look at it, it's hard.

The Living Doll

I paint The Mermaid's face every day before opening. I had taken to painting my own in her tent, cause nobody else would visit her, and she seemed to take an interest in it. So I gave it a shot. It only seemed kind. She's only been here for a month or two, but she still hates everybody. If The Boss's cologne so much as wafts through the flap, she bares her teeth.

The Strongman's been bedridden for a long while now. He's half-delirious from that bite on his arm. He says he hears The Mermaid singing at night. The others want to amputate, but he won't let them. Said he couldn't be The Strongman without one of his guns.

I don't blame The Mermaid. If somebody had tried to swipe me out of my cradle, I'd like to think I'd bite them too. Not that I had to make that call. I was born too-early and too-pale to a set of parents that were too-Godly.

They were too-eager to send me away.

So I relish the feel of The Mermaid's face. I dip a translucent finger into the colored powders and trace the path of an imaginary brow. Sometimes, she lets me paint each wicked claw.

The show's been doing well. We haven't left the coast since the people started pouring in to see THE REAL GENUINE HONEST-TO-GOD MERMAID. Kids love her especially, cause they don't yet know the difference between beautiful and grotesque. I don't think she likes them much. She hisses when they lean in too close.

I won't tell The Strongman, but I hear the singing too. When the night goes black and the people leave, she sings.

The Twins

We hear The Mermaid wailing.

We hear it at night. During the day. In the small hours of the morning. Our tent is opposite The Mermaid's. Even when we sleep, the sound echoes between us like a memory.

On the other side of the camp, The Strongman is dying. He's held on for so long, but he's succumbing. We hear the sea breeze whistling through his lungs, and Gator Boy's pacing. The Boss has been muttering, *Hurry if you're going to.*

How quickly he forgets the man behind the dying, how it's all interconnected. We've been together since birth, our spines intertwined at the base. It's only ever been us.

What family have these men stripped The Mermaid from?

They're shuddering: The Mermaid. The Strongman. Gator Boy.

Barnacles sprout and pop from The Strongman's eyes. He spits up ocean waves. His heart is thundering with the pulse of it.

In The Mermaid's tent, a child's finger breaks the surface of the water.

Somebody gasps. Someone's last breath. Someone's child, pulled into the rowboat. Seawater muffles the crunching, the splintering, the coming apart. How do we sail these savage waters alone?

We cannot.

Gator Boy

The kid The Mermaid tore up gets a grave. We weigh The Strongman's pockets with stones and sink him all quiet into the river one night. It coulda been into the sea, if it weren't for The Mermaid. It coulda been a grave, if it weren't for The Mermaid.

The kid's family went after the Boss. Fair enough. Now just like that, the money's gone. The Boss is fled. The performers are leaving. There's a hundred and one towns for sword-swallowers and clowns to fade into. No place for a green born boy with scales.

Throw it back.

The Living Doll's been feeding it, still. Every morning she dips into its tent with her makeup and a handful of sand crabs or fish. Sometimes, when she leaves, her fingertips are stained bright as birds. I see the sign: THE

REAL GENUINE HONEST-TO-GOD MERMAID. I try not to hate a thing true to itself. People have hated me for less.

Throw it back.

It's twilight when I come for The Living Doll. She doesn't say anything when I appear, only smiles. You can see her teeth through her lips. We go to The Mermaid.

She cups its slimy shoulders and sings lullabies under her breath. It flinches and recoils when I touch its tail. Fair enough. I part the spines, as gentle as I can, and take a better hold. It relaxes, only slightly, and we hobble through the tent, down the lane. The sea is calling, and we struggle through the sand to meet it. Somebody's crying. It might be me. Maybe there's salt in every person's veins.

We dip into the waves. Ankles, calves, waist. When I let The Mermaid go, the Living Doll sobs once beside me.

She doesn't need to.

The Mermaid is back. Its arms are crawling with foam. It reaches up to touch her face. A wave swells. Breaks. Pulls them under.

I am alone.

The Mermaid

We collect shells. Fish. Kelp. We are sinuous and strong with the sea. Along the current, I sing to them of my capture, of the many faces of humans.

I am glad this one came with me.

She waits on an island. It is a big island, with green plants and warm sun. When it is dark, we meet in the pull of the surf, among the crests of fallen waves.

I sing, and the human smiles. She is small and whiter than bone.

I paint her face with fish blood. Dust the corners of her eyes with iridescent scales. She says something, but I do not know what.

Something human, probably.

BOAT

by Heath Mensher

Edie spilled the drink on her shoes. The triple-sec would stick her toes together, but Kris was taking up all her headspace. Oversized sweatshirt and Docs and an *"I don't care what I look like"* aura. It was charming *before* Edie's second kamikaze. It was almost too much to handle now. She leaned against a metal pillar, the sharp studs sticking uncomfortably into her back. The studs were everywhere, lining the walls of the ship's basement. *"They call it the Hold,"* she thought to herself, as the cavernous space began to rumble, the engine loud, the tacky floor vibrating. But people yelled out, matching the rumble, and everyone sensed that a special night was beginning. Edie saw it in the way everyone looked at each other, and the way everyone looked at her. She wasn't used to being on the receiving end of looks like these. Friendly. Happy. The bass kicked in hard, and the crowd assembled on *The Esca* began to bounce.

The majority of the Captain had been eaten. His right eye socket, his wrists. His trunk looked like a bitten apple, the edges of the wounds shiny and uneven. His face showed pain beyond death. The ship's wheel was fastened in place with a bungee cord, the dial set Ahead Full. On the floor, the blood that pooled in the spaces between the rivets double-pulsed with the engine and the music.

"What is happening?"

Kris laughed, and even through the walls of sound pressing in on Edie, she could hear the rich sound. Deep and flushed.

"I don't know?"

Edie laughed too, everything focused on Kris's forearm leaning against her ribs. Edie broke eye contact with Kris's jawline and saw that Neem was near the bar, dancing with someone who wasn't Liam, and that seemed off. Dancing hard. "Should we hit up the next floor?"

Kris was in Edie's ear, pointing to the wide stairs.

"I guess?"

She followed Kris past two people hugging and grabbed the massive rough-rope knots that made up the stairway handholds. Halfway up, there was a moment where she stood between two places, two atmospheres: EDM from below pressed against Industrial above. When she hit the top step, percussion gave way to crunching guitars, and she felt lightheaded. It was darker up here and humid, with too many green and blue lights making faces look like oyster flesh, pearl-wet. But Kris was holding her hand now and that was everything. The insides of their fingers touched and moved, and they flowed to the pleather sectional set against the wall of the iron hull and sank down.

It had eaten until it was sick. It threw up, and ate again until it was full. It was lust and rapture. It threw up and kept moving through the boat.

Kris was half leaning on her now. The music fluttered the air. Sound throbbed and the humidity swelled. Edie felt Kris and watched everything with perfect contentment. Glassware covered the bar, the tables. Most were full. The bartender was smiling at the barback, and the couple standing at the bar were touching foreheads. The numbing guitar shifted to thumping Fela Kuti, but the people didn't move. They were rooted, and the humidity made them appear melted against each other. A man and woman were so close that their eyeballs touched, tiny tremors in the wet whites sliding back and forth over each other. Edie slow-brushed the room with glassy eyes, each new sight a low piano note in her head. Someone stood against a pillar, their head bent back beyond what their neck could hold, sharp bone forced through the skin near their ear. Liam stood awkwardly, the front of his pants soaked and getting darker. Neem stood near the hatchway. She was doubled over, her hair covering her knees, the tips of her middle fingers pressing the sticking floor. Something was sniffing at her hand. Edie couldn't understand it. So she didn't.

There were two on the ship. When they first boarded they'd moved fast, their discharge displacing air like hot grease. It issued before them from skin flaps that pocked their trunks, bacteria filling spaces with sopping heat and oppressive indifference. Now, though, they were sluggish, with distended fish bellies and eyes bulging bloodshot from the force of their vomiting. They did not need to compete, so they did not acknowledge each other when they passed in the halls of the ship. They did not touch, and would not again until they slipped below the surface with their effects.

Edie blew saliva bubbles as she breathed the heavier air. Her eyes moved in their sockets to take in Kris, perfect Kris, dewy and shining. People had sunk to the floor around her. A group formed a pile near the bathroom. *"They call it the Head,"* she thought.

One girl in the group was buried underneath five others. Her silver pumps were sticking out, and a part of Edie knew the girl couldn't breathe like that and had suffocated to death. Kris's sweatshirt was so damp against the open neck of her dress, and Edie was almost delirious with affection for her. She thought of their lives, laced together by nights and meals and the beauty of time wasted together. Edie told Kris she loved her through a thin line of spittle that built at the corner of her mouth and ran down her chin. Edie's hand rested on Kris' stomach, but her body did not move.

The boat chugged on with its Christmas lights and loud music, leaving the Long Island Sound behind and roaming into the deeper Atlantic Ocean, the engine grunting and chuffing, unable to keep up with the new stress from the chop of ocean water. Two bodies spilled out across the stairs leading down to the main deck, steaming in the brine. Oblong feet left prints in the expelled puddles at the bottom of the stairway, reflected in the blue-green floodlights leading into the lounge. They were methodical in their search, and what they didn't need, they ate and ate.

Edie watched them move through the crowd, seeming to touch and squeeze everyone they approached. They seemed to consider and appraise, lifting arms and pressing on chests. Listening at stomachs. Each person they passed was bitten into, the sucking sounds inaudible under the thump of the Buddha Bar track, but Edie could imagine them clearly enough. Their mouths punched into skin and teeth scratched, bone on bone, and they were immediately drenched in blood and bile. She saw them pause before they moved on. They became still. Then they opened their mouths and clotted liquid shot forth violently, their swollen bodies deflating as warm, wet clumps added to the now-steaming atmosphere of the boat. Rail-thin again, they continued on.

"What is that?" she asked Kris without moving her lips. She watched them wade through the ship, hands grabbing air and rubbing it into their shining bodies. "What is this feeling?"

Edie felt completely present at that moment. Her choices so natural, her motives so authentic. She felt wildly free and validated. She was looking for something, and it was here, and she would find it and finally settle into her life. Her body felt a hand on her stomach, and a wave of relief broke over her.

There was a bleating, and the two huddled above the girls on the couch. One removed the body laying half on top, absently checking size and muscle before rolling her onto the deck. They looked down, and before they even touched Edie, they knew.

Edie had never seen bioluminescence in real life. *"It's so much brighter than I thought it would be,"* she thought, joyful at the chance to be here, flowing down and down. They had covered her in something. *"They call it a sausage skin,"* she thought with a silent laugh, and her warmth was sincere. Down, down, as the water grew tight around her. Dragged through dust and sand and chutes running beneath the muddy floor, long and narrow and branching into cavities. She was laid in a shallow depression in the sea floor, bottomed with red sea sponge. Her eyes stayed open, and she could feel them settle on top of her, feel them twisting and folding and never breaking contact, while she fluttered and trembled.

It had been months. The best months of her life, she knew. She was safe - she *made* them safe. She was soft like foam, and free of gravity. Her belly was whipped curds, sunken and smooth, here and there dotted with ruptures, some loose and empty, some with breaching heads. She saw that one near her breast hadn't moved in hours, and felt a powerful remorse. But even so, she felt wonderful, because she knew she would last long enough.

psychopompós
by Samantha Ryan

My father had been dead for exactly fifty-seven days. Today was day fifty-seven, but it felt like day two. I spread my feet apart to steady myself as I adjusted to the gentle rock of the boat, trying to force myself to be in the present.

"You ever done this before?"

"Yeah," I reassured the man looming over me from the dock, "tons of times."

"By yourself?"

I looked over his shoulder at where my dad stood, shielding his eyes.

"Well, no, it was like my dad and I's thing. We would go on a deep-sea fishing trip. Every summer. Just the two of us."

"Okay," he said, uninterested.

"He's actually here with me." I couldn't stop my eyes from glancing at my smiling father. I raised my backpack.

"His ashes. I mean. That's kind of the goal, here, with this boat ride."

My father gave me a look I couldn't decipher, which I found odd, since his expressions were simply manifestations of vague memories in my brain. I created him, so why wouldn't I know?

I could hear my voice fading as words kept tumbling out of my mouth. It felt stupid, but there had to be a ton of people who created this kind of ritualistic closure ceremony to release their loved ones into the ocean. I couldn't be the first person on a journey of solace who had rented a boat from this man. Though, I was probably the first one taking both the dead body and the dead soul with them.

"I hope you find what you're looking for."

"Thanks," I said as he tossed the rope inside the boat and walked away.

My father effortlessly hopped into the boat and began moving around to inspect the quality.

I felt less nervous without someone watching me and quickly started the routine as I moved about the stern, preparing for departure. I could hear his voice as I went – check your lines – and check your motor.

"I know, dad," I said out loud.

I had all my gear, a cooler full of drinks, and more food than I needed for one night. There was still a solid five hours before the sun would set and I could get started.

I pushed the throttle and cruised at a steady pace out of the marina and into the open water. I hadn't planned a specific location really, just someplace where all I could see was the bright, blue, endless ocean, no matter where I looked. I wanted to feel as isolated as possible to say my goodbye. My father leaned across the railing, eyes closed, inhaling every breath of the ocean breeze. Or at least he would have if he were alive. He had been dead now for fifty-seven very long days.

"It's about patience."

I didn't care much about fishing or patience, but spending time with him was what I really wanted, so I focused all my energy on taking in the words coming out of his mouth.

From where I stood on the teak deck of the boat, he loomed over me, explaining step by step how fishing worked. That's what he did for a living – explain things on television to people who valued his opinion. He had gotten so used to explaining things that he couldn't stop when he wasn't working. It drove my mother crazy.

"Do you understand?"

I nodded.

I found myself nodding at the memory. It felt like yesterday, but also today. He had been dead for fifty-seven days. No one prepares you for losing a parent. You feel responsible for the absence of something so great in your life, even though they are the ones who taught you how to shit on a toilet like a normal person. He was just gone. And now he's been with me, day in and day out, for fifty-seven days without even really being here. It was him, but it also wasn't.

"Are you going to stop at some point and put your line out?" he yelled across the ocean noise.

"Yeah, dad."

"You're passing up all the prime real estate."

It was something my dad would have said, but this wasn't my dad, since my dad was dead.

After roaming a little longer, I stopped in a spot to try my luck at some fishing. I secured the lure like he had shown me and tossed my line into the water. It wasn't the same. It felt forced in some way, trying to recreate my childhood as an adult, like visiting your high school after graduation hoping to feel the same feeling you did back then. He stepped around objects he didn't need to avoid and watched me as I worked, but remained silent.

I reeled a few fish in before sitting in the plastic seat, watching the ocean around me. The silence wasn't as calming as I had hoped it would be. Moving to the back, I grabbed a beer and enjoyed the cool rush down my throat. Though I was alone, I felt more self-conscious than I should have, and every now and then I glanced in his direction. He stood, arms at his sides, watching, making sure I didn't screw it up.

"You have to be okay with it dying."

I squirmed, unsure of whether or not it was okay to let him know how scared I was at the thought. This fish had been swimming only minutes before, unaware that anything was about to happen. Then, he took hold of the bait thinking he was getting an easy meal, and in an instant, everything changed. He was yanked, painfully, from his home, suffocating air collapsing his gill slits with every gasp he took. On the deck of the boat, he had to have seen us watching, waiting for him to die. It was the last thing he would see.

My dad smashed the head of the fish on the deck; its innards spilled around us.

I learned later it wasn't necessary to do that.

I wasn't okay with it. Any of it.

It didn't bother me at all anymore.

As an adult you understand that fish die, everything is food for everything else, and shit just fucking happens. Nothing you can do will change that.

I smashed the face of the fish under my foot and felt unnecessary rage as I did.

"Good job, son."

My father had been dead for fifty-seven days. Nothing could change that.

My coworker Evan had looked me in the eyes and told me that, in time, the loss would get easier. He shared how his dad died of cancer and how hard it was to slowly watch him fade into nothing in the end – a shell of the human he had once been.

I wanted to tell him it wasn't like that for me. That my dad was fine until he wasn't. And none of us knew what was coming before it did. That, like the fish, he was there until he wasn't, and none of us knew why. He explained things for a living on the television. The sun was sinking toward the endless edge of water, and it finally felt like the right time to say goodbye.

I pulled the little ceramic jar from my backpack and moved to the edge of the boat.

"Dad," I started, "I hope you found what you were looking for."

I saw him cross his arms out of the corner of my eye.

"And fuck you, I guess."

I bounced the container in my hands, surprised at how little a human could weigh.

"I wanted your final resting place to be somewhere special. Where we had good memories of doing something you loved. I don't know, it seems dumb now. It seems like maybe I didn't even know who you were, really. Just the idea of who I thought you were."

It felt stupid and hollow as I said it. I didn't know how to send off someone who just gave up on themselves and everything around them. He didn't either, judging by the strange look that crossed his face as I worked.

In all of his explaining, he couldn't explain away the pain in his mind. The kind that hunted him day in and day out. He kept it inside and only let us know when it was too late to do anything about it.

I opened the container and watched the spray of gray chalk float away. Some of it landed like dust on the water, and I watched the little particles sink below the surface into the depths below. I didn't feel the relief I had hoped for as I watched him disappear into the air around me. I looked around the boat and noticed his spirit was gone.

I tossed the jar back in the bag and sank into the chair with a new beer to watch the last bits of light fade around me. The gentle rock of the boat lulled me into a light sleep. I hadn't slept well in fifty-seven days.

When I woke up, it was completely dark.

The water was so black I couldn't tell where it stopped and the endless stars began. A solid wall of nothing stretching in front of me, consuming anything that came too close. I raised my hand, worried, but also curious. If I let my fingers leave the perimeter of the boat, would I be taken by the darkness around me, slowly fading into nothing?

There was a blank world all around. Every direction I looked was a vacuum of light and matter. Up above – an empty galaxy. Down below – a dense layer of dark water.

I heard them before I saw them. The waves rippled around the edge of the boat, and I raised a lantern to see what it was. Beneath the water were hundreds of massive sharks moving as a pack in one direction. It was both breathtaking and horrifying. Being so near to these machines of death made my knees weak, but watching them slide through the water with a sense of purpose also calmed me.

Every few seconds, one of the dorsal fins would breach the surface, and I could hear the gentle slap as the sea's shining plane broke in front of me. One of them broke away from the others and turned back toward the boat. Others followed, and soon the boat was the center of a cyclone of quick, dark bodies looping around and around underneath me.

"Shit," I muttered as I moved to get another light.

When I turned, I saw my father, standing on the deck, watching me carefully.

"Fuck," I yelled. "What do you want?"

He watched me but said nothing.

I felt a sudden movement as one of the sharks looped a little too close and hit the side of the boat. My eyes flicked from my dead father to the water, unsure of which problem to deal with first.

Wild thoughts began crashing around my head, like maybe I had died while asleep. Maybe somehow this boat was taking me into the same darkness that had consumed my dad. Or maybe I was here on purpose to deliver him across the river Styx–a ferry into the underworld. Appointed as Charon by Hades himself in this ocean of eternal night.

The ideas were crazy, but my panic was real as I silently watched the sharks turning again to make another approach. I began to think of my own fragile mortality out here on the open sea. No one even knew where I was. I knew if I were eaten by these creatures it would be days, or maybe even weeks, before any guesses were made as to what my true fate was.

Since his death, I had avoided the idea of death at all costs. There is a heavy layer of mortality in dealing with a parent's death – knowing you're next – but with his end, there was so much that I had simply packed away in boxes as we went, unable to load them with more weight than I could lift.

"Dad?" I asked. "Dad?"

He stood at the rail of the boat, staring into the vast expanse of water around us. He looked like he was zoned out, somewhere else completely.

"Dad?"

Finally he turned to look at me and smiled, but it was the kind of smile that made me uncomfortable. As though he knew something bad was going to happen. I wasn't sure what I had done wrong, but whatever it was, I was certain he would tell me.

It happened all the time, this disassociation which I could now see for what it was. But back then, it was just me being ignored. Me thinking it was all about me.

Here in the darkness, facing monsters from the void, hell, or somewhere in between, I felt like I had no choice but to surrender my own feelings of death to the universe around me. I leaned over the edge of the boat, wondering if I could see in the darkness. After these weeks of mental distress and sadness, here, alone, I would slip into the vacuum that had consumed my father.

Slowly, I fell backwards onto the deck, looking up at the specks of stars above, feeling the gentle rock of the boat increase with each loop of the sharks around me.

"I'm sorry," I said to the night. "I'm sorry I couldn't help you. I didn't know how bad it was. For you, I mean."

I could feel the hot stream of tears on my cheeks despite the shivers that went through my core.

"We never talked about that kind of shit, you know? You never told me when shit was bad. I just...didn't know."

I felt the tightening of my chest I'd felt nearly every day the past few months anytime I thought about finding the dead body of my father in his bed, with enough pills in his system to kill the sharks that were now stalking me. That tightening feeling got worse as I heard the splashes of the heavy beasts around me. They were closing in.

"You're going to have to kill it." He said, his voice close to my ear.

"How?" I asked the void, eyes still closed.

"You've got to figure it out, or it will figure you out."

It was one of his favorite sayings. Every problem had an answer, he told me regularly. He wasn't wrong; every problem did have an answer in the end, even if it wasn't the one you really wanted. He had found the answer to his final problem in death.

I had thought for the past few weeks that his answer was cowardice. That somehow it was the easy way out. But now, in this moment, facing the monsters from the deep, I understood my father's need to control his own fate. In the face of certain death, one way or another, it felt peaceful to be the deciding factor.

I could make a choice; I could choose if I were going to live or not. I looked over at my open backpack and decided that I would choose to live. I would make a choice he felt he couldn't.

"Ok." I said out loud. "I can do this."

As I looked into the depths, I could see a fin on the move, headed directly toward the boat. Now was my chance.

Turning, I grabbed the arms of my unsuspecting father. He looked surprised only for a moment before I used his weight against him, shoving him forward and over the rail. His body splashed loudly in the dark. I squinted as I saw the sharks dart wildly around their new toy.

I watched, horrified, as jaws clamped slowly around his body – the sickening crunch echoing in the silence around me. Despite the darkness, I could see mangled chunks of flesh and bone falling from rows of jagged teeth. Pieces of my father drifted around the boat as he was consumed, bit by bit.

Raising one of the lanterns, I saw the last piece being pulled to the bottom. The sharks trailed downward into the deep toward his final resting place like a flock of birds off to find their next nesting ground.

Something hit my feet, and I looked down to see the empty urn of my father. Grabbing it, I stood and moved to the edge of the boat. I threw the urn with as much force as I could. It sailed across the now still waters, and I relished the plunk as it made contact with the shiny surface.

I pulled out my flashlight and did a sweep over as much water as I could, but nothing was there. No ripples or disturbances of any kind. Still cautious, I pushed myself over to the chair and sat down with the light in my lap. I was alone on the deck. Despite the adrenaline pulsing through me, I felt a sense of relief I hadn't felt in a while and found myself drifting into a solid sleep.

My eyes opened to bright light when the sun peered over the endless horizon. I was relieved by the sight of a new day. I began to question if it was all in my head, if the sharks had been part of a bad dream.

Slowly, I stood and looked around the edge of the boat. There was nothing there to indicate my struggles, and I knew if I told anyone they wouldn't believe me. Silently, I prepared myself and the boat for the long ride back to the marina. Once there, I could see the man who had helped me the day before standing on the dock. Nothing had happened to him; he wasn't changed as I was by the underworld.

I tossed the rope to the man as he watched me with an odd look on his face.

"You okay?"

"Yeah," I responded.

"You have trouble out on the water?"

"No, nothing bad."

He watched me pick up my backpack. The weightlessness of it surprised me though it shouldn't have. I climbed up the ladder, silently observing him glance over the boat.

"Did you say goodbye to your old man?"

"Yeah," I said as I stepped onto the dock. "He's part of the ocean forever now."

My father stepped out from behind the man with a smile on his face. The tightening in my chest returned.

"What's the matter?" the man said, looking around in confusion.

"Nothing."

I hadn't let him go or he hadn't let me go. I wasn't sure which was which anymore. My father had been dead for exactly fifty-eight days. But today felt like day two.

A Night Aboard the *Andua*
by Michael Conrad

The two sailors held Syd's arms tight, their broken fingernails biting at her skin. There was no point in resisting now. Maybe she should have when they were still below deck. It's not like the crew had much reason to chase after her, anyway. They'd almost reached their destination. The silhouette of the island was visible in the moonlight, and its welcoming lantern glowed as bright as ever.

Maybe she could have stayed hidden a little longer. Or maybe she wanted to get caught.

The door to the captain's cabin had been removed, probably by the bank. It was blackwood or rosewood, something far more valuable than the rotting oak planks that somehow still held the ship together. The *Andua* hadn't been in great shape when Syd purchased it a decade ago. But it was seaworthy then, and apparently it was still seaworth now, captain's door be damned.

Without it, Syd had a clear view of the man who stood in the cabin. There would be no suspense, no cautious knock by a timid sailor, no dramatic reveal. The moment Sydney had been dragged to the deck, she knew who was in charge of the *Andua*. Her *Andua*.

"Sydney." The captain stepped into the doorway. He didn't gloat, or even sound surprised.

"Mehmet." Syd tried to keep her voice level to no avail.

"It's good to see you again." His voice was strained. He was lying, like always.

Syd replied with a scowl. Mehmet may not have caused all Sydney's problems, but he was certainly responsible for a few of them. He had been the first of Syd's supporters to turn against her, one of the many who had held up her world.

"We'll be disembarking soon," Mehmet said. "We'll row you back to shore with us, but I won't take my chances trying to hide you from the port authorities. You will be arrested."

"I don't want to go back."

That got a little reaction. He probably figured Syd had been living on this ship all along, ever since she lost her home to the same bank that took the mahogany door. There were rats to catch in the bilge, maybe even a few fish to hook at night. It wasn't far from the truth.

"You understand where we're going?" Mehmet asked.

"Of course I do."

"Then you know you can't stay on this ship."

"And you know I can't go back."

Mehmet shook his head. "I can't leave you here."

"Do me this one last kindness," Syd begged. She was a beggar now, after all.

He stared for a long time, his expression placid, but Syd had learned how to read it long ago. It was pity or guilt. Probably both.

Mehmet's gaze shifted to the masts. The wind was dying down and the tattered sails didn't have much left to grab. Still, the ship was moving directly toward the island. They were close enough now that Syd could see a man holding a glowing lantern.

"This is close enough," Mehmet said, not to Syd but to the sailors holding her. "Load the skiff."

Syd was released. She followed the crew to the rowboat that hung precariously over the edge of the *Andua*, suspended by ropes and cables. The sailors climbed in, and Syd was left alone on the deck.

"Will you lower us down?" Mehmet asked. He handed her his lantern.

She nodded. The sooner he was gone, the better.

Mehmet grabbed her hand. Their eyes met, and for a second, Syd forgot that she hated him. But the second didn't last.

"Take this," Mehmet said, touching a small vial that hung on a chain around his neck. Inside was a translucent tincture. He'd worn it since the day she'd met him. "A drop of this will kill an elephant. The whole thing will kill the herd."

Syd didn't want it or need it.

"Just pour it on your skin. It'll get into your blood within seconds."

She wouldn't take the easy way out.

Once Mehmet realized this, his hand moved away from the vial and he said, "It was good to see you one last time."

She'd heard enough. Syd turned her back on him and used the crank to lower the skiff over the edge of the ship. Once it was free from the pulleys, she moved to the stern to watch it row away. Soon, the patter of the paddles on the water fell silent. She was alone.

Mehmet had been the first captain she ever hired. She'd never trusted anyone else with the *Andua*. Together, the ship and captain had made Syd a lot of money. That was all gone now, and she had come to terms with it. But the loss of Mehmet's friendship, maybe more than friendship, had never felt so poignant.

She turned, planning to head to the bow to watch the approach of the island and ponder the possible fates it held for her. But the island was gone. She couldn't spot it anywhere on the horizon.

After a frantic few seconds, Syd noticed the light coming from the captain's cabin. It hadn't been there before. It was the light of a lantern, and it was held by a pale hand. She wasn't alone.

Rumors of the strange island had persisted for centuries. It would appear out of nowhere, only visible at night, and any ship that approached would never return.

Syd believed the rumors. She was just a kid the last time the island had appeared. Her father, a well respected captain in his own right, hadn't believed any of it. To dispel the myth, he took his ship straight to the island one night. He never returned, but neither did the island. Not until recently.

It was the townsfolk who added the extra level of superstition. After her father's disappearance, they said that the island required a ship as some sort of sacrifice, that a kraken lurked in the waves around it waiting for a prize. Even if they were wrong, nobody was going to miss the *Andua*.

"Hello?" Syd approached with careful, deliberate steps, holding her own lantern high. The stranger didn't move. She looked around again, trying to spot the island, but it was definitely gone. "Who are you?"

Once Syd was a few steps away, the stranger came to life. Every part of his body seemed to move at once, as if he wasn't sure which action to take. He settled on lifting the lantern. "Sydney my girl. Is that you?"

The voice sent ice down Syd's spine. It was so warm, so familiar, but impossible. She was close enough now to see the stranger's face. His skin was bleached and sickly, hanging loosely as if it were a size too big for his body. His eyes were empty tunnels, the sockets drooping to fill them.

But even without eyes, Syd knew who this man was. At least, who he was supposed to be.

"Have you finally come for me, Sydney? I always knew you would." The voice belonged to her father, but this thing, this abomination, was something else entirely.

"What trick is this?" Syd demanded. "What are you? What's happening here?"

Her father barked out a laugh. "I know what's happened to you. The life you led, the empire you built. I'm proud of you, girl. No one who sails these seas hasn't heard your name."

"Then surely you know the rest of the story," Syd said. This doppelganger wanted something from her, and whatever it was, she wasn't going to give it away.

Before she could press him, there was a splash near the stern and then the sound of water dripping onto the deck.

"Who goes there?" Syd called, spinning around.

"I know the rest," her father's phantom said behind her. "A few bad deals, a little too much greed. And then you got scared and placed too much faith in someone other than yourself."

Syd still wasn't looking at him. Another figure had appeared. She watched the newcomer draw closer. He was suspended in the air, gliding across the deck, water dripping from his boots.

It was Mehmet.

Unlike Syd's father, the captain still had his eyes, but his skin had already begun to sag, and his grisly pallor made him glow in the lantern light.

"You know it was only business, right?" he said.

Syd thought back to Mehmet's wife and the fever she'd contracted. How the captain had begged her to make port, to find a doctor. But they'd been behind schedule already, and Syd had refused. At the funeral, Mehmet said that he didn't blame her. But he did. What followed, the destruction of Syd's empire, had been more than just business.

"What is this?" Syd growled, turning to face her father again. "What manner of specter are you?"

"Poor judgment," her father said, rising into the air, his inhuman legs drooping beneath their own weight. "Even the krill, frail as they are, know what hunts them. You have no place on the sea."

Syd never believed the tales of a kraken. But she had to acknowledge some mystery in the disappearing island. And now, there were dead men, floating through the air. It was easier for her to believe in some foul sea monster than ghosts.

She lunged forward and grabbed her father's ankle. He darted away, breaking free from her grip, but not before Syd saw the string that gave the grizzly marionette its flight. It wasn't the tentacle of a kraken holding her father's corpse aloft, but a cable, stretched taut. This was all some macabre trick.

She turned to face Mehmet, who was now only a few steps from her. "Is this your doing? One final act of revenge? Have you not taken enough from me already? Are we not yet even?"

"I told you before, this is just business."

"Then end my life now," Syd cried. "No more of this torment. I'd apologize a hundred more times if I could bring her back for you. You know I would." Her cheeks were wet, and it wasn't from the spray of the sea. "You know I can't."

Mehmet's face stretched into a vicious smile, but he said nothing as Syd's father descended beside him, still suspended from the cable.

"He believed you," her father said. "I'm not so cruel as to leave you in want. He knew of your regret."

Syd stared at her father's corpse. Her fear and guilt simmered together, fermenting into rage. How dare Mehmet desecrate her father?

She lunged, this time reaching for the cable instead of the corpse. It pulled away again, but Syd was faster. Her fist closed around it, wet and slimy from the spray of the ocean. The body rose into the tangled mess of rigging, taking Syd with it.

"I suppose it's time to show you the truth," Mehmet called, still on the deck.

"I know your truth Mehmet," Syd called back. "And I can't blame you. You'll go to the grave despising me. But to torment me like this? It's sadistic."

"You are wrong in so many ways. His last thought was of how to save you."

The cable Syd clung to thrashed wildly, shaking both her and her father's corpse free. But as she fell toward the deck, her lantern's light swept past the edge of the cable. Only, it wasn't a cable at all. She glimpsed feelers and spines wreathing the tip of a tentacle before it disappeared into the black sky.

Syd hit the deck hard, pain erupting all along her back. Her father's body hit in a different way. It wasn't solid like it had appeared. A soupy mass of flesh and fluid splattered on the wood and bled into a sickening mound. In the puddle, Syd saw worms, no longer than her finger, emerging from the ooze and wriggling their way across the deck toward the ocean.

This was no theater production. And it wasn't the kraken from the townsfolk's imagination. Such monsters ate sailors whole, ship and all. At least, that's what they did in the stories. No, this was a parasite. A bottomfeeder. Something that gorged on its victims, savoring every last drop, until there was nothing left.

As Syd stumbled to her feet, Mehmet watched, wearing a grizzly smile. She could see the slimy tendril holding him aloft.

"Do you understand now?" he asked.

She did. None of this was Mehmet's doing. Mehmet, and the rest of the crew, were dead.

"What is the island?" Syd asked. "Just an illusion to lure us out here?"

"It is indeed a lure," Mehmet said. "But no illusion."

Alongside the ship, there was a rush of water. Something rose from the depths, reaching high enough to block some of the stars. Syd took an uneven step toward it. And then another.

She raised the lantern and recoiled in disgust. The thing the townsfolk called an island was really a writhing mass of worm. At first, she thought there were many worms, but it was all a single creature knotted together with no clear beginning or end.

"So, what do you think?" Mehmet's body asked, a puppet to the whims of the worm.

Syd ignored the question. This creature wouldn't keep her alive much longer, and there was nowhere to run or hide. She'd only get one chance.

"If you kill them, then how do you know their thoughts and speak in their voices?"

"I take all the blood within a few seconds," the worm replied with Mehmet's voice. "That's what I need. But most of the instruments are all still here. His brain contains the thoughts, and his mouth and lungs can still produce the words."

"And the other sailors?"

"Dead, as is Mehmet. Your father, too, kept preserved for my little ones."

Rage like nothing she'd ever felt before burned inside Syd. Everything that happened in her life seemed meaningless now. Nothing could be more important than killing this creature.

"Why do any of this?" Syd said. "Why am I still alive?" She turned her back on the body of the worm and walked toward the animated corpse of her oldest friend. "Why torment me?"

The other end of the worm, the one that had been holding her father, wriggled across the deck at incredible speed and pierced Mehmet's body, just below his chin, the tip disappearing into his head. Not a single drop of blood appeared around the wound.

"I know their last thoughts," Mehmet's voice said. "Every one of them thinks of themselves in their last moment. Except these two." Mehmet's arm rose to point at the pile of mush that had once been her father. "Both of them thought of you, thirty years apart. I thought you must be something special."

"So I'm just a curiosity to you." She'd closed the distance and stood right before Mehmet's body, still suspended in the air by the worm.

"I'm sorry that I have no grand truth for you." She was close enough now to feel Mehmet's breath. It was cold and stale. "Are you ready for the end, Sydney?"

"Just one more thing." Syd leaned in and kissed Mehmet's lifeless lips. It took every ounce of her willpower not to retch, but she needed to block the worm's vision of her hand. If it could speak with Mehmet's mouth, then it could see with his eyes.

When she pulled away, the vial Mehmet wore around his neck was in her hand. She turned away, flipped the lid back with only the slightest motion, and let several drops fall onto her skin.

Even in the moonlight she could see the liquid soak in. She didn't feel a thing as the tincture contaminated her blood, but she remembered Mehmet's words: it was enough to kill a herd of elephants.

"You know, in a different life, I could have loved him," she said.

"He loved you in this one," Mehmet's voice replied.

Syd felt a prick at the back of her neck as the worm wriggled under her skin and then pain all over her body as it drained her blood. Then she felt nothing. With her last thought, she wondered if the mass of the worm's body weighed more or less than all those elephants.

Sea People

by Katherine Traylor

When high tide floods the town, the Sea People emerge from the surf to visit the shops of Main Street. There aren't many humans on the streets: most of us take refuge in upper floors until the waters recede. But we watch them from our windows: the mermaids with their iridescent skin, the Drowned Men, the Hags. Others, shyer and more secretive, shroud themselves in sailcloth or plastic as they stumble around the waterfront, seeing the sights.

They're tourists. They buy keychains at Sea Breeze Gifts, point at the crumbling churches, and gorge themselves on hush puppies and seafood. You're not supposed to eat much fish now, but the Sea People seem to enjoy the novelty of fried food.

We're alarmed at first. It's an unforgettable experience when a Drowned Man (asking for directions) takes you by surprise. But we soon learn they're all basically harmless. It takes time to get used to their smell (fishier than fish, with a hint of blood underneath). They always stand just a bit too close, mimicking human manners just well enough to be uncanny. They dress in rags and scavenged garbage, if they bother wearing clothes at all. And they'd rather stare at a cat for hours than give a human the time of day. But they only come when the tide is high, and they pay with gold and pearls, so we're able to tolerate them pretty well.

But the sea keeps rising.

Soon Main Street is permanently flooded, sunken houses echoing with a constant slop of water where water never slopped before. We leave them to the Sea People, who move in right away—as if they'd always lived in houses, as if they weren't scavengers profiting from our losses. Most of them don't interact with us at all. They set up their own businesses, selling each other trash and fish and chattering in ugly voices that were never meant to sound above the water. They carry their children in plastic bags, spin kelp twine on the wheels of drowned bicycles. Such uses they make of our broken things, repurposing our town's wreckage for themselves.

The mermaids are the boldest: more active than the Hags, less fearful than the Drowned Men, more able to breathe on land than other things that scuttle beneath the sea. They like to sit on the roofs of sunken houses, looking over the water. Perhaps they're homesick. But they stay.

Our children find them all fascinating. Our daughters bring home sharp-toothed girls with fishhooks in their lips.

Fish Gather to Listen

Our sons tryst with Drowned Men (the beautiful, tragic ones who still have most of their flesh).

We try to caution them. We forbid them the shoreline. But the lure of the forbidden only draws them more quickly.

Whispers abound of human children dragged underwater. More substantial rumors tell of clients occasionally failing to return from the flooded Pearl Hotel, which the mermaids have turned into a brothel.

Tensions rise. We try to drive them out. Occasionally we succeed. But they always come back.

It makes you shudder to hear one coming up behind you: wet fins or clammy feet flapping on the sidewalk, and the grunting puff of breath you hear from the ones who aren't used to breathing air. Much worse are the quiet ones, who make no sound at all. Some of them only appear as shadows at twilight. Finding one behind you is enough to stop your heart.

Even the placid Sea Hags are eldritch, though. And nothing chills your blood like the song of a mermaid at sunset. It's a tragic, eerie, hopeless sound: a mourning for lost homelands, lost history, lost love, everything a drowning sailor might think of in his last moment alive.

So the town dies piece by piece, falling into disrepair, then into decay. People die or move away, and no one's having children to replace them.

No one but the Sea People. There are new children now, green-skinned babies running down the weed-slicked sidewalks and diving into the water. Their parents peddle seafood hand-caught from the deeps, working from sunken storefronts, their prey kept alive in underwater storerooms till they sell it. Even the humans buy from them now. Our fishermen are rotting with the buildings, dying one by one, their graves in the tide-threatened cemetery mostly unvisited.

And we've had enough.

Tonight, we drink too much. Piling into a leaking boat, we patrol the town's dark waters, readying our weapons. We'll take it all back, or die trying.

It's late and dark. Our feet are soaked. A wet salt mist pervades the air, as if the water had drawn a curtain around itself for privacy.

The Sea People are hiding. This makes us angry. Our bloodthirst grows with every minute left unsatisfied. Finally, we see a lone shadow moving across a storefront: a Drowned Man, out for a late-night stroll. We can't see his face, but the shuffle is distinctive: the careful walk of one trying to keep his body from falling apart.

Someone cocks a gun.

"No," says someone else. "Fire is the surest way to kill a Drowned Man."

Someone picks up the gas can.

The mist closes around us, covering our faces like wet tissue. The Drowned Man vanishes like smoke. Perhaps he was never there.

The water under our feet is getting deeper. The boat is sinking. We scramble for the sides, but something catches us.

Under our screams, a wet chewing sound begins. In the boat's flooded bottom, little jaws are working: widening the hole, hastening the sinking. As we're pulled under the water, something beneath us begins to eat our feet.

Our Yellowed Bones

by C. C. Rayne

They say the pier is built from the bones of drowned men. Ryland doesn't know if he believes it, but he still likes to spend his evenings there, feet dangling as he stares at the silver sky. Each night when the sun sets and the ocean swallows it up, there's a brief ghost-span of darkened moments before the moon pops out in its place. *The lying time, the dying time,* the village men call it, or simply *the time between right and wrong.*

For Ryland, it's the only time of day he gets any peace. His father is hard at work sewing sails all through the night, so he can't catch his son breaking the window latch to sneak off to the beach, can't take out his fury on Ryland in short, sharp bursts. It's easy to climb the rusted ladder onto the pier, its yellowed struts draped with seaweed. Over the years, Ryland has hidden here from his father more times than he can count.

Three days after his twentieth birthday, the merman emerges. Ryland watches him surface from the murky, green water; his heart accelerates at the strange apparition.

He runs his eyes up and down the creature and notes the glossy curls of his hair, the way scales shimmer along his spine like shards of glass.

"You're not human," he says to the merman, staring down over the edge of the pier.

The answering grin is filled with sharp shark teeth.

"And you *are* human. Do you have a name?"

"Ryland," Ryland says automatically, then bites his lip, unsure if he just opened himself up to some sort of magical spell. Fey folk steal your name, don't they? Perhaps merfolk do the same - though that's not what they're famed for in the hushed whispers of the town. He hasn't spent too much time in the taverns and the tailors' shops, but he's heard the muffled words of the men all the same. *The ones from the sea, they eat hearts and they steal skulls. They take what they want from us, and build cities out of our bones.*

This merman looks to be about his age, though. And he's smiling. And he's...handsome.

"I'm Lyre. It's a pleasure to meet you, Ryland, especially upon such a lovely pier."

"Is it built from human bone?" Ryland says. "That's what I've always been told."

"Do you always listen to what you are told?" Lyre asks. The moon, rising from the horizon, is reflected twice over in his eyes. Twin points of silver glint alluringly up at Ryland from the dark expanse of the waves.

Ryland stares down at Lyre for a minute longer, until there's a brief shift of rock and silt from the abandoned beach. He whips around, panicked, ready to run if his father has come to drag him home.

When he returns his gaze to the sea, the merman has dived. Only bubbles and ripples remain, muddying the water. Rainbow light shimmers on the surface like an oil slick.

The temptation to dive in after him is...strong. Instead, Ryland steps off the pier, down onto the sand, and kneels to look at the base of the supporting pillars. The yellowed struts feel glossy and smooth when he runs a finger along them. They are each pocked slightly in the center with a long, bony groove.

He comes back a few nights later. It's hard to see clearly in the starless, ghost-spun dark, but when he makes his way across the beach, Lyre floats in the water. Waiting for him.

"It's bone," Ryland says, with as much confidence as he can muster.

"Yes." Lyre smiles and swims further out, moving to the place where the pier terminates and the lawless waves take over. "Feels good to make discoveries, doesn't it?"

"Have you killed anyone before?"

The words escape before Ryland can consider them. Once again, he finds himself afraid. *The ones from the sea, they're unpredictable,* the men in town always say. *They take what they want, and we never know what they will do.*

But Lyre simply smiles, and smiles, and smiles. There is nothing gentle in his shark-tooth smile. There is only wild love. Or maybe wild hunger.

"Yes, I've killed quite a few humans," he says, in the same tone with which Ryland might ask for a cup of tea. "Humans have killed quite a few of us."

Ryland wants to stay on the shore. Or - he knows that he *should* want to stay on the shore. Land is where it's safe, where he'll be protected from storms and merfolk and the dangerous unknown.

But the beach sand grates and gnaws at his bare feet. His father's face burns angrily across his mind, and he has to run away, or run closer, or at least run *somewhere* new. So he steps onto the bone-built pier and keeps his feet moving until the pier falls away beneath him.

The ocean wraps around him with a muffled whistle of impact. Ryland resurfaces, blinks water droplets from his eyelids, and hacks sea-salt from his lungs. His ears are clogged and his clothes are soaked. He feels cold. He feels miserable. He feels endangered, or perhaps he simply feels dangerous. It's a surprisingly good way to feel.

But when his vision finally clears, Lyre is gone.

Overhead, silver light splits the horizon. Ryland floats on his back for an hour more, one hand wrapped around the supporting bones of the pier. He waits, hoping fruitlessly for arms to reach up and embrace him from the deep, but the merman does not return.

There is no time to sneak away to the beach during the next few days. It's easy to notice little things around town, though, now that Ryland knows to look for them. The wind-chimes at the barber's shop are made of small, pointed shark teeth. The fine embroidered waistcoats at the tavern are stitched with glossy locks of hair. When Ryland goes to visit his father at the shipyard, he steals a look at the billowing sails which hang from newly-built merchant vessels. Their edges shimmer with scales, each one selected by a careful craftsman's eye.

Bile rises in Ryland's throat. He doesn't bother locking the window latch behind him when he sneaks out that night.

Lyre floats far out in the bay, buffeted by rough and raucous waves. Ryland walks straight into the water to talk to him.

"My people have been killing merfolk this whole time," he says. The weight of salt and seaweed on all sides makes his chest seize up. He scrabbles pitifully at the waves, arms pinwheeling to stay afloat.

"Oh, imagine that, you've noticed," Lyre replies. "Believe me, we certainly have."

The merman's mouth is razor-edged. This close, Ryland can see it's not a smile anymore. It's simply a void, waiting to swallow what it needs to survive.

"I don't blame you for -" he starts to say. But before he can finish, a wave washes over his head, and he is left coughing weakly for air. The merman circles him, fins carving smoothly through the murky expanse while Ryland struggles to inhale.

"Please understand that I don't ask for forgiveness," Lyre murmurs under the clamor of the sea. His ribs flex, muscles starkly visible beneath the scale-flesh of his chest. "It's nothing but a construct of yours, and I don't care to adhere to it."

Ryland tilts his head backwards and wonders how long it has been since the merman ate. And *what* the merman eats. Those yellowed bones on the pier had to start with some flesh and blood around them, didn't they?

"Then I won't forgive you," he manages to choke out.

Lyre's face shifts, half-shadowed, eyes keenly focused on Ryland as he drowns. He doesn't look like he's planning to intercede in any way. For some reason, that truth stings more deeply than the lack of air.

"I'll just...understand," Ryland says desperately. "I understand why you take from us...the way that you do."

"Then you know that I *could* take all the bones that I want," Lyre whispers. "But, how much of yourself are you willing to give?"

The waves grow bigger and bigger. There's a final, thunderous crash of water against bone, and Ryland gasps, losing the battle. Water seeps into his lungs; his arms fly up and he slips underneath. Down, down, down.

Drowning is a bright thing. The ocean is crushing him to pulp and shreds, but in the pressure, there's a strange sort of hunger. Something like love.

There is no moon, but that doesn't seem to matter. Here in this cathedral of green, Lyre's eyes glow, twin pinpricks of sickly white light.

Their eerie bioluminescence pulls Ryland ceaselessly forward through the murky water until his limbs finally tangle with Lyre's. Their lips collide. The world stutters to a stop.

Suddenly, there's no longer any need to breathe.

The porch light is still on when Ryland steps through the front door of his house hours later. His father sits at the kitchen table, a sewing needle clutched in hand. There's a violent fury in the man's face that would have made Ryland run and hide in his younger days.

Now, though, he is much more dangerous. When he smiles at his father and runs his tongue along his teeth, the molars are sharklike and sharp.

That night, Ryland hauls a sail filled with bloody bones to the beach. He drops them into the water from the pier's edge, watches as each one splashes into the waves. He waits as the sun is dragged down in a last gasp of violet and ochre.

No moon appears over the horizon. But Lyre does. The merman stares up at him from the water, face filled with gratitude and disbelief. Bones bob in the tide's eddy, but their red stains are already being scoured off by the sea. Soon, they'll be yellowed and smooth, strong enough to support any weight.

"Let me build with you," Ryland says.

The merman's smile is bright enough to set the ocean aflame.

Singing Sweetly Through Your Veins

by Tiffany Michelle Brown

You awaken to the sound of a planet dying. Waves crashing on the beach. The discordant strains of an out-of-tune violin. The hum of a bumblebee. All fused together into a single symphony that is both terrible and achingly beautiful, the kind of sound that burrows under your skin and takes up residence in your blood.

Beneath the song, your temples pulse in time with your heartbeat. Your throat is dry and feels brittle as tissue paper.

Need...water.

But you can't get up to tend your thirst. In your head, you roll to the side, stand on sleep-stiff legs, and amble into the bathroom for a sip from the tap. In reality, your body lies completely inert atop starchy sheets in the cheap motel Marcos booked for your trip.

Maybe you need to start smaller. You try to wiggle your fingers, but can't conjure so much as a twitch. It's as if all the electrical signals in your body have short-circuited.

Are you having a stroke? Some sort of neurological episode? Are you dreaming?

You test your vocal chords next. You concentrate on what you'd like to say—Marcos' name over and over, simply to get his attention—and will your mouth to open. There's pressure in your lungs, proof of the effort radiating through your chest, but your mouth is a closed vice.

Panic burns hot as a furnace in your stomach. You need help, but how the hell can you get it if you can't move?

Okay, you can't speak, but maybe you can *hear* Marcos. If you know what your friend is doing, perhaps you can shift your strategy. To what, you don't know, but you have to start somewhere.

You imagine your ears are oversized antennae. Is Marcos deep asleep in the next bed? Watching TV? Up texting that cute surfer girl he met on the beach this afternoon? You hope to God he's still awake and might intuit that you're in trouble.

Despite your efforts to tune into the sounds around you, all you can hear is an overwhelming *crack* over and over, mixed with haunting notes from a string instrument, the rush of water. These noises are but a whisper in the dark, the volume low, but they dominate your hearing.

Has some ocean water pushed through your ear canal and leaked into your brain? No. All your equipment was airtight earlier in the day, fitted in place in accordance with all safety measures, so that doesn't make sense.

Your perspective changes suddenly. You're now sitting up in bed, staring into the darkness. In your periphery, a soft glow pulses.

What in the actual hell? You haven't instructed your body to rise. It's simply decided to—of its own accord. But at least you're moving now? Perhaps your body is waking up.

Can you turn your head to the side?

No.

Flex your fingers?

No.

Frustration blooms in your chest like ink. Your mind is sharp, but your body—

The dingy mattress groans as you stand, another movement that is completely out of your control. Something is very wrong here. You scream for Marcos, howl with a primal urgency, but the hotel room remains quiet, your cries locked within your brain.

And then the music swells—wings and strings and destruction and water—crashing upon your consciousness, drowning out your horror and—

Isn't it beautiful to be the witness to the end of something? To hear a song written just for you? To zoom through the air no longer beholden to gravity? To feel the sublime power of Mother Nature?

The symphony is yours. Let go. Take it in.

The song dissipates, and you return to the dark hotel room. You're in the bathroom now, standing in front of the mirror, pulling your wetsuit over your hips. Your reflection is a nightmare. If you could, you'd be wailing. An intricate network of neon pathways threads through your hands, arms, chest, and neck, anchored just below your skin. The winding conduit is your circulatory system.

Your reflection's bioluminescence winks at you, vibrating with energy, not unlike stars hung heavy in the night sky.

The rhythm, there's something familiar about it.

Your hands, controlled by an unseen puppet master, zip up your wetsuit, snagging some of your skin in the process. The pain is sharp and immediate. You swoon inwardly though your face remains stoic, blank in the mirror.

As the pain ebbs, you fix your gaze on the steady pulse in your neck. Despite the obvious connection to your circulatory system, the rhythm doesn't reflect your heartbeat.

The tempo...it matches the *crack, crack, crack* in your head. The drone of bees creates a sizzling bass line. It's the song, which means...There's something in your veins, and it's...singing?

Waves caressing your body with salt and surf. A melody you've never heard before lands on your tongue. It is a warm hug. A nectar-tinged susurration. A gentle lullaby.

Wet sand squishes between your toes. You take jerky, labored steps toward the shoreline. Whatever is controlling you doesn't understand how your body is meant to function.

You know you're going into the water. An air tank is strapped to your back, your oxygen regulator jammed into your mouth. But why? Are you meant to discover or retrieve something? The thought makes your stomach roil. Midnight swims are difficult, even for experienced divers with high-quality headlamps and intimate knowledge of the reef. The ocean is murky and mysterious at great depths even without the added shroud of nighttime darkness. If this *thing* wants you to find something, you'd have better luck searching during the day.

But of course, your zombie-like movements would be conspicuous and strange in daylight. Someone would intervene, and that wouldn't do, now would it?

You gaze at the horizon as you plod into the surf. Frigid water bites at your ankles like angry fleas. The moon hides behind a blanket of clouds, and you can no longer make out the point where the night sky meets the sea. You're simply wandering into darkness.

When you're waist-deep, the song takes over. Your body is flooded with warmth. Your eyes close for the first time since you awoke to this living nightmare, and the blindness is strangely comforting. You pretend you're asleep, dreaming, lulled into REM by a chorus of string instruments—

Stravinsky and Bach and Mozart and Brahms and Mendelssohn and Beethoven and Tchaikovsky and Bartok and Paganini and Shostakovich and Vivaldi and Bruch and Sibelius and Prokofiev—all playing at the same time. Air dusted with rosin. Calloused fingers plucking chords out of the air. A tapestry of sound so thick and warm and intricate and...

Water scuttles past your face. Your legs pump in a steady rhythm, propelling you forward into the small pinprick of light created by your headlamp. The further you descend, the louder the beckoning song becomes.

You're going to the source. This sudden revelation should breed fear deep within your chest, but instead, your mind spins with curiosity and fascination. What on this planet can make such exquisite noise? What type of being has poisoned your blood? You know you're about to witness something awe-inspiring, something you'd never discover on your own despite your love for adventure and commitment to never do the same dive twice.

And isn't that the point of venturing under the sea? Wild encounters. Otherworldly sightings. The feeling that you are but a small and insignificant part of something much larger. Something you'll never truly know or understand despite your zeal for exploration.

There's a part of you that wants this.

A jetty of coral comes into focus. Lush, orange branches snake from a human-sized hole in the calcium deposits. The sight is familiar. You'd discovered this very opening earlier in the day and had trained your lights into the inky depths of the cave's maw to see if you could traverse it. Underwater spelunking is "too hardcore" for Marcos, but you live for the thrill of discovery, the inherent danger of getting lost or stuck but always managing to find a way out.

You'd leaned close, peered into the hole, half-expecting to find a refuge for eels or a small shark. But it had been empty. Calm.

And that's when it got you. Sunk its teeth in.

Now, a ghostly song sings sweetly through your veins, and something you can't explain controls your movements.

You sail head-first into the underwater crevasse. It's a tight space, and your knees crash into rock as you kick, propelling yourself ever forward. Your shoulders snag against errant bits of coral. The pain registers in your body, but you can't do anything about it. Can't cry out. Can't adjust course. Can't flinch. You must endure the abuse and continue on, pulled forward on an invisible string.

The rock surrounding you is full of song now, vibrating, as if you've entered an underwater club where the power of bass rules all. Even the water shivers around you, and you can't decide if it feels like you're trembling or being rocked to sleep by a supernatural being.

The tempo has increased considerably, and all the dissonant parts of the song are bleeding together. The resulting noise resembles a high-pitched scream.

Something grating and terrible, and yet, you're still entranced by it. There's a thread of beauty running through this car crash of sound.

As you venture onward, your sight is suddenly and inexplicably overlaid with the image of a planet cracking in two, a thunderous affair that buffets you with space detritus, sonic energy, and sorrow. You feel a swarm of bees enter your ears and set up an industrious shop within your skull, their collective drone a steady homage to their queen. Then, you're surfing, threading your fingers through the foam of a wave as it breaks upon itself, the rush of the ocean filling your ears. A violinist stands on a street corner in a tattered coat, running their bow over strings so rapidly a cloud of rosin surrounds them.

Suddenly, the sound is snatched away. Its absence is harrowing, and you feel the lack in your marrow. It's like being sucker-punched, emptied of agency. The desire to cry, to gasp, to walk it off negated by the shock to your body and nervous system.

You've stopped swimming. You've exited the tunnel, and you're bobbing in a vast cavern. The coral surrounding you is unlike anything you've ever seen, an intricate maze of rock painted in vivid greens and pinks and yellows. The vibrancy of the cavern walls is a testament to how far below the surface you've swum. You're locked away in a box of coral, a container that's never been subject to the brutal bleaching powers of the sun.

No one could find you down here, no matter how hard they tried. The thought comes to you unbidden, and you push it away. That kind of thinking isn't helpful now. It'll only increase your fear as you face the inevitable: you're not leaving this place.

The wall of coral in front of you begins to quake. It cracks in two and separates horizontally, revealing a jagged pattern that resembles—

Teeth, you think. *Those...are teeth.*

As the coral jaws open, revealing a pitch-black expanse, a new sound snakes through the water and wraps around you. It transports you back to the kitchen of a shitty diner, the kind of place that slings congealed pie slices and burnt coffee. There's a haze of smoke in the air, thanks to the over-greased flattop. A waitress wearing a checkered apron has dropped her tray. Five white bowls that once held piping hot chili are scattered in shards across the floor. The sound of china breaking reverberates through your ears. For others, the sound is one of alarm. It's an indication that something has gone awry. But you've always liked the sound of plates and bowls shattering— delicious, clean demolition. There's something strangely beautiful about it. Something magnetic.

Though the nostalgic, grease-covered reverie dominates your vision, you're acutely aware of the sensation of being pulled forward. Water bubbles past you. The temperature grows colder. The sound of breaking dishes sings through your veins, a bittersweet, inescapable dirge. It grows frenzied, manic energy searching for a way out, for a release.

The pain is excruciating as your veins rupture, and warm, wet music spills through your insides. But the shallow cavities of your human body are not enough. The song is building, ready to crescendo. It requires space.

As your body bloats and your skin stretches, you imagine yourself a balloon and the sea a curious child who wants to see just how far latex will stretch before it pops. Meanwhile, the dishes continue to crash inside of you, a personal violence that desperately wants to be made public.

It happens quickly, the tearing, the destruction, the separation of skin and sinew and bone and matter. You watch a ribbon of gold shoot through the water. It scurries deeper into the cave and joins a larger network of spun strands of sound. The whole network flares, lights up, ignites.

Sings.

Sings.

Sings.

And it's beautiful, this predatory underwater chorus.

Your final moments are strangely peaceful, painted in awe and acceptance, saltwater and symphony. There's something comforting in knowing you've become a part of something grand and wild and unexplainable.

Your search is over.

Starfish

by Billie Karras

It was cold in the tent and Ashley, laying all the way at the other end of it in a heap of old blankets and clothes, was no help to Cheryl at all. She shivered and hugged herself instead, trying to squeeze some warmth out of her chest and into her arms, but there was no heat to be had on a night like this. She didn't really want to touch Ashley, anyway. Not these days. Not at night.

"I wish we could have a fire," she said softly, mostly to herself.

Ashley grunted, apparently still awake. "No wood."

"I know that." Cheryl sat up, wrapped a flannel around her shoulders.

"Where you going?"

"I wanna watch the stars."

"It's even colder out there," Ashley said.

"I know." Cheryl unzipped the tent and stepped out into sand, feeling the cold of it bite her toes. The sound of the sea was louder out here. She loved that sound. Always had. Especially when she could listen to it whisper through the open window of the apartment they'd shared together. But that was long gone.

Beneath the crashing of the waves, she heard rustling in the tent. Then Ashley was beside her. She had her arms crossed tightly around her chest, her hands shoved deep into her armpits. Cheryl couldn't see her face; the moonlight wasn't quite bright enough for that, but she could feel the trouble that lined it all the same.

"It's coming on again, isn't it."

Ashley didn't reply. Cheryl knew what that meant.

"You gotta stay away from the others this time, okay Ash?"

"I don't wanna talk about it."

"*Promise* me. We'll figure it out. I have some money, and if it's not enough I can steal something, but you can't do *that* again."

Cheryl realized Ashley was crying now. She took Ashley in her arms in spite of herself and kissed her cheek. It was like ice. "Hey, baby, shhh," Cheryl whispered. "It's gonna be okay."

"It hurts," Ashley said. Her arms were still crossed. Cheryl tugged at them gently, and after a while, Ashley let them out.

They were covered in round, smooth bumps on one side. Cheryl knew that, in the light, they'd be pale shades of pink. On the other side, where the soft skin on the inside of her forearm should've been, rows and rows of thin, soft tubercles had sprouted like some strange form of alien hair. They sucked softly at her fingers like a million tiny mouths.

This is so bad, Cheryl thought. When they'd first met, when things had seemed so fresh and miraculous and beautiful, it had just been flare-ups that Ashley had brushed off as nothing more than an odd skin condition; just a few bumps here and there, once every few months. But now–

Cheryl shuddered, remembering the last one. That had been just a few weeks ago. She thought about how she'd lost Ashley for a whole night. How she'd gone around town, desperately searching for her. How she'd finally found her, under the pier, hunched over an old angler fisherman. His frozen look of horror. His running, melted flesh. The sucking sounds.

But she didn't want to think about that.

She didn't want to think about that ever again.

Ashley had stopped crying. She was staring at the stars. Cheryl kissed her again. Her skin tasted like salt. "It'll be alright," she repeated, and didn't know if she was talking to Ashley or to herself.

Ashley sniffed, then was silent.

Cheryl kept one arm around her, and at some point they found themselves sitting together on the sand. The sun was beginning to rise in the east now, and the city behind them began to glow purple. Soon the sea would glitter with it, like so much amethyst in a million roiling hydrothermal veins.

"You wanna try to get some more sleep before daytime?" Cheryl asked.

Ashley didn't respond.

"Babe?"

Ashley's eyes were glossy, blank. Cheryl grew alarmed. She shook her. "Ash! *Ashley!*"

"I'm not tired," Ashley said suddenly, and Cheryl jumped. Ashley still wasn't looking at her. Then Cheryl's eyes widened. Fear wormed through her every orifice and bit, hard. She couldn't move, could only croak a hoarse–

"*No.*"

From the thin pooch of Ashley's stomach, something very much like a large fist had begun to push out against the inside of her shirt. The fabric hissed, smoking, and the smell of burning cotton stung at Cheryl's sinuses. Ashley turned to her, and Cheryl saw tears running down her cheeks again.

"I'm *hungry.*"

And then Ashley's hands were on her, gripping her thighs with fingers that seemed to grow longer, longer, digging in, holding her in place.

"Stop, stop, please *stop–*"

But Ashley was on her now, wrapping her arms around her body, curving them bonelessly as if they were a large, crusty pair of snakes. As they wound over her shoulders, Cheryl could see that Ashley's fingers had melded together, making dull points at the ends of her hands. The tubercles were like a million tiny, suckling needles against her skin. Cheryl screamed and, finally unlocked from her fear, tried to get away. Ashley's grip was too tight. The smell of burning fabric was nauseating. And then it *really* started to hurt.

The bottom of Ashley's shirt had burned away and the bulbous, jellylike thing pouring from a hole below her sternum squished against Cheryl like something out of a storm drain. Cheryl shrieked as the flesh beneath her chest began to melt away. Ashley's eyes rolled back into her skull and her forehead stretched upwards with a wet crunching sound- growing and growing and finally settling into a point like the ones her hands had become. Behind them waves crashed and overhead gulls cried, and beneath it all were Cheryl's screams.

They dwindled to sobs as Ashley ate her intestines. Cheryl thought of a school trip she'd taken to an aquarium once. They'd let all the children hold the starfish. She'd thought they'd been fascinating, pretty little creatures. She'd thought the same thing about Ashley once. What was happening? It was absurd. She could almost feel the painful shards cut into her brain as her mind began to splinter.

Then, blessedly, an idea came to her–

She was *dreaming*- of *course.* It made sense. The stress of living life this way, hungry, homeless, the anxiety of it all- yes, of *course* it wasn't real. And not just this- the entire last few weeks, the fisherman Ashley had eaten- all a dream. And Cheryl would wake up soon. And it would all be nothing but a fuzzy, poorly-projected ghost of a memory by the time breakfast rolled around, and she wouldn't even remember enough to explain it in any way that made more than the vaguest bit of sense. Would they wake in their tent, she wondered, or–?

Excitement prickled her guts even as Ashley slurped them away.

Could she, perhaps, wake in the apartment they used to share? Was the street-living they'd resorted to during the last few months part of the dream? Oh, god. She couldn't wait to find out.

Minutes passed. The pain dulled. Everything dulled. She didn't wake up. Cheryl was colder than ever, and wished again to have a fire. She searched for at least one star in the rapidly lightening sky. She didn't find it.

"Please," Cheryl whispered to her love. "It hurts."

Ashley didn't seem to hear. Tubercles had grown out of her face, making it hard to see her eyes, her mouth. But when her head lowered, leaning up to Cheryl's face, allowing the tubercles to brush against her lips–

Cheryl knew that she had.

I'll be waking up any minute now, she thought. *I'll wake up and I'll be next to Ashley and she'll be herself and I'll tell her I had a horrible dream and she'll hold me with normal hands and she'll kiss me with a normal face and she'll tell me everything is alright.*

Cheryl smiled at the thought. If there'd been anyone there to see it, however, it would've looked more like a grimace.

More time passed. Everything was very gray now. She did not wake.

Ashley's distended, jellybag tumor of a stomach was fully inside her now, feeding, hollowing her torso out like a pumpkin at Halloween. Cheryl stopped wishing for fires. She stopped searching for stars. Her sobs had long since been replaced by weak murmurs. She thought about where they would go for breakfast once they woke up. They had a few dollars- certainly enough to splurge on some McGriddles. She decided she'd buy them orange juices as well. And hashbrowns, oh yes. And if they awoke in the bed they used to share, in the apartment she'd been sure they'd lost? Good God. Cheryl would weep with joy.

She'd take Ashley to brunch. The fancy place they used to frequent with the crab cake benedicts, the black truffle goat cheese grits, the bottomless mimosas, yes, she remembered it well. They would eat like queens. They would laugh. They would tip monstrously. And then, they'd go back home and take the love they shared and fall into bed and giggle and sigh and make some more of it.

And everything would be alright.

She'd been wheezing, but when the bottoms of her lungs finally began to dissolve and she still hadn't woken up in their old bed, whole and in love and alright, Cheryl stopped making noises altogether. After that there were only the waves, the gulls, the beachy morning breeze.

That and the sucking sounds.

Topside, Topside, Do You Read Me?

by Amy E. Casey

I don't know how long I've been alone down here. I am so weary of being wet. The computer is dead. There are records, dates and times, and numbers in my handwriting, but I can barely read them anymore, as my head is so heavy, and every time I breathe, my vision shakes. The words *research station* are important, and I cling to them. I am a scientist. A researcher. A team was recording me, in hopes that we could sell a show about the expedition. Maybe I'm still being recorded. But my mind seems broken, and I've stopped talking to the cameras. As I said, I don't know how long I've been alone. The matte, pelagic nothingness of the deep sea is just on the other side of these glass walls. I fill my days with staring out at it, waiting for it to do something. My wet hair clings to my neck. I smell awful.

The moisture is a problem. There is a long cut on my hand and it won't dry. The skin around it is white and dead, frilling around the raw, pink flesh of the wound like a mushroom. Condensation beads on every surface: the walls, the floor, my glasses. I wipe them off, sliding the lenses across my wet shirt, a smearing that does little good. I feel small inside my pressurized dwelling. It's tight quarters. A box, really, suspended in the sea, small trails of bubbles always rising from the metal seams of its construction, because nothing is ever truly airtight, is it? There is a tube of silicone to patch the seams when water seeps in. It's half squeezed out, and I wonder how long it can last.

Down here, I am on the very edge of the reach of the sun. In the daytime, I can sometimes see shadows, but visibility is murky as the seas swell. There doesn't seem to be much of anything alive out there. I believe we've had bad weather. My carbon dioxide meter emits a shrill beeping sound in warning. It always accompanies me. I hardly hear it anymore. I have a radio, but I've stopped calling on it every hour, afraid to run down the power. I still try a few times each day. I hate the way my voice cracks as I try to say clearly: *Topside, topside, do you read me?* The familiar crackle of static is all that comes through in response.

There is a square opening on the floor that I could use to exit the structure if I put my gear on, dipping myself into the frigid seawater, but I don't think I can get to the surface without assistance.

I wait for night to come, watching the glass go from dark blue to black. But always, there is the sound of the ocean's movement bedeviling the glass. I weep, blowing my nose into limp tissues. As I said, I don't know how long

I've been alone. I lie in my hammock, swaying above the slick floor, breathing the foggy air, head swelling with the hateful pressure, shivering beneath a damp blanket with a shiny underside, occasionally becoming conscious again of the *beep, beep, beep* of the warning meter as I enter a state much like sleep.

A thundering slam jars my bones as something huge hits the wall from the outside. I reel from the impact. I get down from the now-swinging sleeping hammock, slapping my bare, wrinkled feet to the wet floor. I power on the exterior lights. My dwelling becomes a beacon in the open ocean night, beaming light a few feet in every direction. I peer out, pulse thrumming inside my neck.

The black emptiness reveals a great eye coming into view, white and rotten with blindness. Then, a gaping, toothless mouth. Flaring gill slits as thick as my own body. Dull, wildly fluttering fins. I cannot see the whole of the creature at once, only these small flashes as it turns, circling my glass box. A mad ecstasy floods my heart. I notice bubbles trailing from a new vulnerability in the structure. They rush and shimmer in the light as my friend slams into the wall, knocking me to the floor. I wave with both arms and cry out to him through the glass: *I'm here! I'm here!* I press my palm to the cool pane, wiping the cloudiness away to see him better. The creature's skin rockets upward as he turns, twisting to face me from the other side. The other eye is not so glassy. I believe he can see me with this one. I tell him, *I don't know how long I've been alone.* He makes a sound that I am already forgetting.

I marvel at his size, his two different eyes, the beard of parasites trailing from his rubbery lower lip. But I sicken when I see him struggle to right himself, part of the huge body gone stiff and unmoving, fins on his left side desperately flailing. Failing to find a bearing, he crashes into my dwelling once more with a deafening crack. I wish desperately to communicate with him, but I only see the end of his tail as he loses buoyancy. His body sinks downward, obeying the inevitable pull of the seafloor. I watch until the last shadow of him falls away. So soon met. So soon gone. Another carcass lost to the depths.

A second alarm is going off now.

I hear the rush of water finding new paths in. I feel the whole station start to heave. Whatever I was tethered to, I am not anymore. The lights flicker out.

From Stagnant Waters
by Kathryn Reilly

"...the ruddy cheek and now the ruddier nose
Shall tempt thee, as thou flittest round the brow;
And when the hour of sleep its quiet brings,
No angry hand shall rise to brush thy wings."
from William Cullen Bryant's "To a Mosquito"

Desperation and loyalty drive the woman to the swamp's center, past the blooming spider lilies, horned bladderwort, and Louisiana swamp irises, the developer's notice crumpled in her hand. With wrinkles etching hard years into her skin, she narrows her eyes, seeking the remnants of a murmured legend hidden in the depths of her beloved, ancestral land. Belief corporalizes—at least she hopes it does. Slowing her skiff, she floats among a semicircle of cypress stumps, certain she's found the place she seeks as the air stills. Withdrawing the knife, she slices twice vertically, chanting the incantation passed down her maternal line. Sharp pain quickly fades to a dull pulse as her blood seeps into the murky waters caressing the tangled, green cities of purslane, duckweed, and salvinia. *It's not suicide if it's a sacrifice,* her mind comforts. *I believe,* she thought, *I believe and she will rise.* Her blood swirls, snaking down, down, down toward a skeletal finger reaching to embrace it.

Wisps of consciousness return slowly. Poisoned blood begins to flow beneath mud-caked skin again. Each muscle in the body rebuilds itself, and soon, she can move her fingers and toes. Aware yet unable to move fully, she endures the agony. One moon later she claws her way through the detritus until her head breaks above. She rises: clothed again in sheer ceremonial attire, looking around her beloved swamp. Her left hand reaches out and touches the cypress altar, the lifeblood of the swamp, before recoiling in horror and pain. Mouth opening, brown water pours forth before her guttural scream ravages the silence.

A low, buzzing drone ripples the swamp's stagnant waters, responding to the call. Waters ripple over Baratarian skeletons and half-empty lipstick tubes, transposing a black tube between skeletal fingers. During the city's conception, locals revered the swamp, speaking in hushed tones of the power of the *other* that shivered their skin. But only a few ever ventured in: to bury treasure, to dispose of the dead, to seek lore remedies passed down from shackled generations to freer ones. The swamp accepted all without complaint. Over time, reverence twisted into disgust as the civilized erected a neon city beyond its borders, tempting visitors with liquid comfort and pleasure promises. Reduced, the swamp survived, offering breeding grounds to her chosen who multiplied, thriving and working to spread sickness, keeping the human plague from their home. This gradual transformation dissected the swamp's viscera. Those of the blood simply watched the swamp swallow the city dwellers' trash, breaking it down and transforming it. Every now and then an object just wouldn't fit; it disturbed the stagnant waters, and those appointed removed the item back to the city, leaving it in meticulously kept French Quarter courtyards. They watched Bourbon Street tourists swarm between the bars, illuminated by the many neon lights, oblivious to the progressive sound reverberating in the swamp.

Those within the swamp remember foreboding things, and stay indoors busying themselves. When the swamp air simultaneously stills and electrifies, they scurry, securing fine mesh over every crevice in their homes. At their parents' firm requests, children relinquish play and spend daylight collecting cinquefoil, or five-finger grass, to fill five drained eggs to protect against curses. An egg guards every corner in the home; the fifth stands before the door protecting against undesired visitors—in whatever form they may elect to take. Tradition holds that evil will pass by homes with such a charm.

Many had witnessed the signs of her return: one woman saw a snake upon an anhinga's back; another whispered of lazy, swirling waters deep in the swamp, churning up instead of down. A tale of the ancient sacrifice, a curse too powerful to break, leaves the lips of the oldest generation to warn the ears of the newest. As stewards of the swamp, they protect themselves as best they can. A Crone's anger may survive death, for the swamp holds the power to heal or to harm. Its memory is long, and those living in the swamp honor all such sacrifices.

This evening households sit closely together, the eldest sharing the story of an ancient elemental, angered so by greedy men desecrating the swamp that she called out to the swamp for vengeance and watched as a mosquito landed and drew her blood. As the story continues, the youngest extinguishes all tallow candles shortly after dusk as an extra precaution. Even the youngest knows the importance of blending magic with common sense: one tries never to draw more attention to oneself than necessary. Yet in the city, unaware, the tourists drink, stumbling from one neon god into the bowels of the next.

The veiled figure stands atop an ageless cypress stump deep in the swamp, cradling the body of she whose blood called her. Though weeks dead, the sun dried the body well, except for the bloated and missing skin around the hands and forearms where the appendages had floated in the water. Bending her head, she whispers, "Will you serve me? Will you join my vengeance?" The dead, thin lips part, and a sigh escapes.

"Very well, then." Placing the body on the largest of the cypress stumps, she begins the invocation, calling forth in a language long dead to the world. Clouds part and the moon's rays illuminate the body, caressing it in power.

Removing a sacred knife carved from animal bone more ancient than any artifact, she plunges the knife straight into the woman's still heart. Leaning close, she slices her own arm and urges the blood into the heart until it drinks its fill and begins a slow pump.

"Rest now, my apprentice. Soon I will share with you my knowledge and the burdens of this world."

Knowing full reanimation will take hours, she lays the new being down on the skiff and turns back to the sacred cypress stumps, readying to prepare a new Bloody Mary. Swamp gas hangs in the air, much like how the priestess's words hang softly about her lips, coaxing the swamp to name its transgressors. Enough methane surrounds the area that living souls dare not enter; the smell emanating from the rotting vegetation steers the living in different directions. She cocks her head and listens, enjoying the occasional pop followed by flares of eerie light. She favors this spot above others because of the moonlight filtering through the moss and spindly branches, etching her skin into an erratically spun spider's web. Her sisters all claimed prettier gardens in the world, but she relishes the moist, ethereal nature of the swamps. Their creatures and fauna possess hauntingly beautiful adaptations dry gardens lack.

Standing on the stump, her blood boils as she recalls her original vengeance cry, resounding throughout the swamp centuries ago. She'd watched, enraged, as first French, then Spanish settlers, and finally land barons drained parts of the swamp, hacking her cypress trees for profit. Transporting goods and people up and down the

Mississippi demanded tough wood, and the cypress, nearly rot-proof, was their first choice. Hordes infested the swamp, harvesting the trees. Her people had always revered the cypress for its strength; they believed this tree possessed the strength of fire, that it could heal wounds and souls alike. Her essence existed long before Greek tales told of Cyparissus' grief, and how such grief transformed him into a cypress tree. She was so old now, she couldn't even speak her name, yet she could read the writing on her skin that spoke to her oath of protection. She recalled how foreigners entered this land, and how the people moved away from their roots and into a rootless future.

After the 1788 fire, she withdrew to the swamp's center, calling forth a true corporeal form. She watched in rage, unable to stop the rapid destruction of the cypress giants in the quest to rebuild. Nine of her apprentices followed, all willing to endure the most precious sacrifice. Each stood on the remains of a slain cypress, eyes closed, hands offering a different poison, reciting the protection as their priestess stood behind them and released their blood. It ran in rivulets down their bodies into a stump, which absorbed it fully. The final voice chanted, silenced by her sure stroke. The immortal protectress, with a blade decorated in nine apprentices' blood, consumed the final poison and added her own blood before sinking beneath the swamp, swallowing its water.

Her lands now lay steeped in conflict. She remembers cursing the year Jean Baptiste La Moyne, Sieur de Bienville, founded the city beyond her swamp as a French fortress. Wasn't the city's legacy eternal warfare? Though her warfare would endure unnoticed, unheeded until the catastrophes the swamp suffered were assuaged.

Her own sacrifice riddles her with pain; she'd swallowed poisons that churned immortally in her veins. Night itself cloaks her femininity as she walks upon the stilled waters, honoring each of the nine risen trees by rubbing the wood until a splinter splits her skin, honoring the pain of her followers' sacrifice. With five splinters in one hand and four in the other, she stands regal among the decay, squeezing her fingers until blood wells. Splaying her crimson fingers wide, she blows and watches her blood become a calling mist, beckoning her chosen. The swamp wraps itself around her when she thinks, *Those who destroy nature will be destroyed by it in the end.* The swamp desires many things, but nothing more than its right to thrive. The bloody mist searches every corner and blankets the spaces where thousands upon thousands of her soldiers wriggle, feeling her call.

Sixteen days after their awakening, she watches carefully as a new brood realizes life. When they emerge forty-eight hours later as larvae, she sprinkles more drops of her blood onto the placid waters, enjoying how they consume it. Alert and mobile, her apprentice watches, listening as she speaks of blood's power and of magic so old, it simply lies waiting in the world. In the in-between times, she demands her newest apprentice master words long forgotten, coaxing her through the pronunciations, demanding her tongue and throat move in alien forms. Though the swamp itself has shrunk to nearly half of its original size, its larval horde squirms exponentially, the remaining stagnant waters providing a perfect breeding and nurturing ground for her chosen. They nestle in filth, growing strong, ignored by all except dying lore and legend.

She watches patiently as the larvae shed four times, becoming larger with each molt. She fuels their struggle, her blood commanding persistence as they stretch and squirm, breaking through each old, confining skin. The priestess appreciates their ever-transforming forms; she feels kinship with this insect and its many phases. Her own painful transformation ensures her awakenings as the swamp desires. She's sure that if Lafayette's treasure remains hidden, so too will her watery grave.

In thirteen days, the mosquitos mature from larvae into pupae, doing nothing in particular with their time. They wriggle this way and that, hitting rubber or earth boundaries; feeling confined, they squirm another way, only to find themselves bound. Frustrated, they writhe more fiercely until they break through their skin. They feed sparingly, waiting for transformation into adulthood.

During this stage, the priestess visits the females, speaking to them of her blood and the power it carries: the ability to protect the world from those who would harm the swamp. Walking on the waters, she traverses the swamp, speaking softly to the broods of the blood awaiting them. She explains the destruction of the swamp, how her poisoned blood will strengthen them and weaken others, that though they are small, they could possess death's great power. Hundreds of thousands enter into pacts with her as they reach adulthood. Her promise of longer life and the endurance to fly beyond the swamp carries great appeal; they will be able to fly and taste so many types of blood. Blood sweetened with liquid courage; blood sweetened by sex; blood sweetened by sugars and spices; blood sweetened by fear. Males are worthless as they lack the piercing proboscis for blood taking; their mouths enjoy nectar from common flowers, though they favor the rich reds and golden yellows, flying great distances for rarer blooms. So it has been for centuries: females are both creators and destroyers; life and death depend upon their generosity.

She returns to the altar and waits, her apprentice now mummering the summoning, wind carrying her whispered words throughout the far-reaches of the swamp, her eyes blazing blood fire. The horde emerges, trying their wings and reveling in their freedom. The Risen unclasps her gown, letting it sink beneath the waters. The night itself stills. Elemental skin glistens faintly, pulsing with a power the world forgot; she stands bare save a silver branch curved around her throat. The sacrificial knife appears once again in her hands, and she opens her skin, allowing the scent of her blood to draw them home. Standing quietly, she waits. A wing-created wind rises steadily until she sees flickering lights weaving among the trees, great silver shapes shifting to accommodate the trees and their parasites. Moonlight glints off thousands of wings, and a haunting humming infuses the quiet swamp, reverberating just above the murky waters.

Raising her arms and arching her protected neck, the Risen invites the mosquitos to drink. At her welcome the females descend, thousands upon thousands, each with distinctive, iridescent wings and a thirst for her blood. They fly toward her as one shimmering exoskeleton, singular in purpose. Before partaking of her gift, the insects dip low in reverence to she who offers herself to them. They drink until their bellies engorge with blood. The elemental priestess relishes each proboscis's prick, each tiny stinging sensation. A tidal feast unfolds as wave after wave of mosquitos drink. When they are full, they retreat to rest among the trees. The beating of wings fades slowly until it flatlines, and silence settles over the swamp.

The Risen waits until the last female removes her proboscis, flutters back, and finds a spot on the altar. Her apprentice falls silent, ending the summoning, head bowed deeply in reverence. Knowing her blood will churn within her chosen, driving them near the brink of madness, she smiles. Her blood will drive the strong to feed; the weakest will not survive the poisons—they will fall into the waters, nestle among the rot, and return her blood to the swamp.

Tiny drops of blood cover her entire body, creating a liquid, crimson gown. As one, the insects shift their wings to capture the moonlight and bathe the Risen in a silver glow. She bows her head, acknowledging their respect. She knows within two hours their hunger will re-emerge, more commanding than it could ever naturally be. Their thirst will spur them toward the city initially, where the price will be highest. She proudly recalls the 1853 yellow fever epidemic, claiming 8,000 lives. New Orleans is due. Her chosen will continue transmitting new strains of malaria, yellow fever, dengue, and encephalitis to their hosts all over the South. Then they will breed wherever stagnant water resides before heading north and west and east and south. The priestess closes her eyes and smiles, imagining the coming carnage and confusion that will offer her swamp respite.

Her vessels begin flying through the swamp, over rusted Ford carcasses, and past humble homes protected by belief. Those inside watch the horde pass, speeding beyond the swamp and toward the living dead. The lights of the city shine as a beacon, and the winged wind whispers that just desserts should always taste of copper.

Endling

by Samir Sirk Morató

The mermaid is not faring well this year.

I know because I pass her cove every day that I trek to the foghorn building with oils, tools, and rags. She's eradicated the sea lions who once claimed that beach, so when I peer into the crescent cove from a ledge above, I see only her: a two-thousand-pound behemoth spread on the beige rainbow of pebbles, seething and kvetching, a sea serpent in human costume. A monster fit for wrestling elephant seals.

Now that we no longer land on her beach—now that there aren't any more flipped rafts—it's easier to be fond of the mermaid. Sometimes, between shifts, I lay in the salt grass to watch her. The mermaid has a moist, tuna-gray body, a muscled torso, and the tail to end all tails: a hulking rudder of flesh meant for undersea hunting.

From a distance she appears more human, but it's unwise to believe that the white spots on her face are doe eyes, the streaks on her ligaments fingers, and the barnacled swells on her chest breasts. Her eyes are her supposed pupils, her fingers painted fins, her breasts some bulging part of her swim bladder. She's hairless, but the many spiny ridges on her skull catch trains of kelp, so every day, we watch the mermaid scratch at her kelpy locks. All the boys joke that she wears wigs. Whenever mole crabs are snagged in the kelp, there are jabs about lice.

I used to feed the mermaid. Or try. "Eat up!" I'd say, softballing my rationed sardine rolls toward her. But they'd always bounce off her snout while she snorted in irritation. The birds ate them instead. After my futile favors made me more hungry than happy, I stopped. The mermaid never noticed.

She's nothing like us. That comforts me. I would love the mermaid less if she were another complicated, terrible human. She's lived here longer than anyone. Even the lightkeeper. When I first saw the mermaid, that seemed right. I thought that she fit this desolate island better than any of us. The longer I've stayed, the more out of place she looks. And as I've studied her nubby teeth and scars, I've realized that she's very old.

"Her kind doesn't belong here," the lightkeeper says. "Some scientists I talked to five years back said that our lady is from Hawaii. She must've been migrating through here when that cargo ship sank and made her go oil-blind. Now she can't leave."

I didn't exist when the *S.S. Montebello* sank. Neither did my parents. Although it was swollen with oil, its hull didn't burst during the sinking. When it did decades later, the bay turned black. Half of all we know vanished into that sticky void. All the strange little seabirds, the baitfish, the sharks, the seals—gone.

Except the mermaid.

"Were the scientists interested in her?" I ignore the lightkeeper's sigh. I'm a foreigner marooned here too, but unlike the mermaid, he must talk to me.

"No. They were interested in the extinct local mergals, and not too pleased to see ours." The lightkeeper eyes me. "Are you feeding that crone again?"

"No."

"Good. It's a lost cause."

I grumble as if I've reconsidered feeding her, surprised the lightkeeper mentioned it. I haven't contemplated that for months. It's as alien as thinking we once had our own mermaids.

The bay is pretending to recover. Unprecedented amounts of eggshells and afterbirth webbed the island this summer. After years of starvation, that bounty isn't enough for the mermaid. She's too arthritic to chase sea lion pups, too big to reach into auklet burrows, and too blind to seize cormorant chicks. The anchovies, rockfish, and squid beading the currents aren't filling her stomach. Her ribs are jutting, her ancient oil blisters reopening.

Maybe the fish are too far down for her. Everything's changing. What used to be hot has run cold; what was cold has boiled. What looks well is ill. I know how a wounded refugee perceives these changes, even if she's a seal murderer the size of a submarine.

"She'll adjust," I tell myself on the raft. "She'll fatten up while we're on the supply run. Why wouldn't she? I'm not from here and I've done fine."

If time can fix the mermaid, then time can fix us. Will fix us.

When the boys and I return weeks later, laden with delayed foghorn parts, dry goods, and unsigned renewal contracts, I expect our monster to be glowing. Dried blood from hauling boxes threads my palms when I walk to her cove. Autumn wind whips grit against my boots and overalls. Gull bone dust grinds underfoot. I halt on the ledge.

The mermaid lays capsized on her massive side in the shallows, panting, covered in shell bits and tidescratch. The reek of rotting kelp cloaks her; flies crowd her skin. Giant chitons ooze up her tail. Gulls land on her. She swats at them, hissing, her bleached eyes watering. The gulls halfheartedly flutter away. Like some of the algae-poisoned sea lions across the island, the mermaid is shitting herself to death. The cove is smeared in concentrated fish paste which resembles pumpkin puree. She looks as washed up as the debris around her.

The mermaid won't be here next season. I want to call the scientists, want to suggest that we cut her a blanket of erosion control material or bind her and ship her home, but that's all fruitless. Betrayal scorches me. Then fear. Compared to me, the mermaid is invincible. She's undeniable. How can she possibly die on us?

I turn away from her.

That night, while everyone else snores, I'm sleepless. I creep out of our spider-infested bunk telling myself I need to piss, then end up wading through lupin and darkness with a giant wrench in hand. I don't know how to kill a behemoth. I should at least try. As another unwilling transplant, I owe the mermaid. If we're losing an island landmark, I at least want a say in that process.

The boardwalk catches my boots as I hurry to the cove. The gulls scream; the seals bark; the waves crash. They never stop. I keep my flashlight low to avoid the gull colony's wrath. Its beam splashes against the rustling grass. Ahead, rhino auklets cruise across the walkway, their eyes and horns gleaming before they disappear. I hunch over my bowl of light. My sweat makes the wrench cold.

Wavesound washes closer. Gravel crunches. Maybe I can kill the mermaid with one hard blow to the head. If not, I can't leave her worse off. Wind salts my skin. I shine my flashlight into the cove.

The mermaid lays face down in a blooming crescent of flesh. Tide licks at her sides. A school of not-quite-girls clusters around her like handmaidens. Rockfish fins, plump bodies, and pale, fuzzy skin dance together in the shallows. I see scale patches of canary, vermillion, white, and speckled tan. Our mermaids have bony heads slit with melancholy mouths and are crowned in fin frills. Their eyes are abalone disks dotted at the center. The mermaids shyly stare into my flashlight beam, gills flaring, agape mouths dripping with teeth and strings of flesh, their faces waxy echoes of mine. They already sparkle with fishing line.

Our mutual paralysis stretches. The ruby holes they've gnawed into our mermaid glimmer.

"You all should've stayed gone." When I speak, covered in chillbumps, I hear my feeble surprise. "It's not safe. The worst is on its way."

One mermaid gives an uncertain burble. Seafoam gnaws at the propeller wounds gashing her breast. She's a third my size. They all are. A giant, limp hand lolls in the current behind her. It twitches. I feel nothing for it. The gull and seal screams pastiche into nonsense words: into the fragmented cries of people. A sky of shining eyes watches me from the water.

If I were brave, I could slip into the cove and mercy-kill our mermaid. I could catch some of the new ones. I could kill them out of kindness too, or capture them for the scientists, or untangle them. Our people haven't met for years. I could show them we mean no harm. I could lie.

Instead, I extinguish the flashlight. I turn away from the shoreline and hurl the wrench inland as hard as I can, then stand there, listening, heaving, unsure what thud or uplift in gullshriek means it's landed. The screaming, dark world holds me in its gut. My pulse beats in my ears. I wait to move until I've gotten my bearings. By then, wet sounds of chewing intermix with the waves. If there are real words there, I choose not to hear them. I stagger to bed in darkness without looking back.

When morning breaks, the strange, native mermaids are gone, but our mermaid still lies on the beach. The boys try towing her into the surf, but even with her entrails dented she remains too massive to move, so they agree to leave her ashore until the new ladies chew her into a manageable size. And before the cloud of birds comes, before the reek of fat clouds our coast, I go to the lightkeeper's office. I decline to renew my contract.

Because I am terrible and human, I lied to myself about loving the old mermaid. Watching our dying future eat her revealed the truth: my compassion for her is for myself. What I want is for me. Because neither of us could fight displacement, what I want is for everything that killed the mermaid to go away before it gets me. No kindness will stop that.

So I am going elsewhere, to some landlocked place that only knows grass and dirt. There will be no ever-worsening waves or sunken time bombs. The water will just come from the sky. And if—when—the end arrives, it will arrive quickly. Like oil in the eyes. Like teeth in a spine.

I hope the mermaids forgive me for my inaction.

I pray that I die a softer death.

From The River The Penny Dropped

by KT Wagner

Seven-year-old Pearl didn't believe in magic until one night, deep in the murky waters of the wishing pool, she gathered a gold tooth along with the usual collection of coins.

The river tumbled out of the mountains, its currents swift and cold. Cedar and hemlock forest crowded the bank, boughs dipping toward the water. Each afternoon, Pearl's ten-year-old brother rowed a dugout to the granite outcrop in the middle of the river. He charged tourists a penny each, round trip.

Dressed in a billowing black skirt, hair tied back with rope, Pearl's mother waited on the outcrop. From the shade of a portable canvas shelter, she wove stories for the tourists, but never for the pilgrims. She spoke of answered prayers and miracles. The better the story, the more coins the tourists threw into the still, deep pool.

Mother never told teeth stories. She crossed herself whenever pilgrims arrived and spat if she thought they weren't looking.

No one would ferry pilgrims, and they were forced to swim through the rapids to the outcrop. Occasionally, one drowned. They knelt beside the wishing pool and talked in whispers of a door to another world and wishes granted in exchange for teeth. Rotten teeth; tiny, white, baby teeth; and animal teeth, some as large as Pearl's thumb: they threw them all in.

While Mother spun her tales, Pearl remained on the river's edge and took care of her little sister, Rita. On Mother's instruction, she taught the four-year-old to swim and dive. They practiced in the shallow pools near shore.

At twilight every evening, Pearl, Rita, and Mother visited the nearby tavern deep in the woods, where brother washed dishes and swept floors. While the girls waited outside, Mother paid the cook a few pennies for partially consumed table scraps. They returned to the river, where Mother and Rita ate, but Pearl had a job to do first.

"Don't pick up teeth," Mother warned, as always. "They aren't worth anything."

Pearl felt sure that wasn't true, but Mother walloped her if she asked questions. Besides, she never glimpsed any teeth in the gloom, just coins.

Pearl swam to the outcrop, fighting the current. She arrived exhausted. In the dark, she built a campfire on the edge of the outcrop and thought about food. She thought about food a lot.

Then, she dove into the wishing pool to collect the day's coins.

A glint of gold reflected firelight at the bottom of the pool. A tooth. She'd never seen a gold tooth. Surely Mother would want it. Fist tight around the prize, she kicked toward the surface and the glow of the campfire.

One last rocky ledge to avoid—

A creeping, slimy touch on her thigh. Heart pounding, she pushed away.

A tentacle circled her neck, dragged her back down. She clawed at its rubbery skin. Suckers slithered across her face and fastened to her lips, stretched them wide. A tentacle pushed into her mouth. Water filled her throat. The tentacle yanked out a molar, then a second one from the other side.

Pearl screamed into the water, and the creature flung her toward the surface.

Gasping and choking, she hauled herself onto the rock. Blood poured from her mouth, hot on her chin and dripping black in the moonlight. Rushing water smothered the sound of her sobs.

"Get back in that water." Mother gestured with swipes of her fists.

Pearl cried that she was hurt and scared.

"Dive or I'll send Rita," Mother yelled.

Pearl shivered in the muggy heat, remembering the night her older sister became stuck in the narrow gap at the bottom of the pool. The next day, divers pulled her, lifeless, from the depths. Mother didn't claim her body. And that night, Mother sent five-year-old Pearl to dive in her sister's place. Pearl could barely hold her breath long enough.

Staring at the water, Pearl tried hard to shake the memory. Stomach tight with hunger and fear, she fought to bend her knees, to flex her feet and dive. Her entire body shook.

It was like Rita and her older sister stood beside her, holding her back. Holding her up.

Pearl considered the tentacle. Finally, she slipped thumb and forefinger past her tongue, squeezed another tooth, and pushed it hard toward her cheek. The pain. She was sure her jaw would snap off. She pulled the tooth out.

Whispering her wish, she tossed the bloody offering into the water.

Mother's screams echoed for a long time.

Pearl hugged her crying sister. Then she gathered Rita's hand into her own and led her home.

The Blood We Carry

by Annemarie Bennett

The first time I see a dead body, I am four. He's in bloody pieces and looks less like a man and more like a broken doll. Momma is tossing bits of him into the pitch-black waters of our property's lake, the one I'm not allowed to step foot in. The darkness goes down and down, swallowing the body whole. Gramma appears from behind the big, old oak tree. She hums a song that I can't make out from our little house's patio. Its melody hovers in the thick air.

It's Momma who realizes I've been watching. She panics and looks Gramma in the eyes. Gramma just nods, wrinkles folding into themselves. Momma approaches me like I'm a fawn about to run, but I stay frozen in place. My chubby hand grips the arm of the baby doll I tugged outside with me. Momma reaches me in my haze and kneels before my tiny frame.

Blood taints her flannel nightgown and gloves her hands. It sits under her fingernails. She almost places a hand to my face to comfort me but stops right as her fingers ghost my cheek. She is paying me courtesy by not tainting me with the blood yet. *Yet.*

"You weren't supposed to know," she murmurs. "You're too young."

"Momma, what is that?" I didn't know he was a man. I didn't know he was a person at all.

She croons over me, "Shhh. Go to bed, baby. Go to bed."

She turns to look at Gramma, but she's busy tossing the last bits of body into the waters. Her hum still lingers between us. "Go to bed baby," Momma repeats.

I do as she says because I can't think of doing anything else. I peek through my blinds and watch as the shadowed forms of Momma and Gramma hold hands and sway by the waters.

The first version of the nightmare starts with me suspended underwater, unable to breathe. The sound of Gramma's humming fills up my ears with water. One by one, my limbs are slowly hacked from my body. The sound of my bones breaking apart fills my ears with water. I try to scream, but Momma places a blood-stained finger to my lips, still hacking off my remaining leg with her free hand.

It's Gramma who tells me the story. I am ten. We sit across from each other at the kitchen table over brightly colored cereal one sunny morning while Momma is at work. Normally this table is reserved for school lessons, but for now it's summer, and I'm meant to be innocent and free.

"Eva, I think you're old enough to understand something from long ago. You're too young to know according to your Momma, but I didn't sugarcoat our lot in life for her, and I won't for you either...no matter what she says."

We have an unspoken rule to never discuss that night. I shut my eyes, and memories flash before the forced dark. Blood. Bits. Momma. The melody swaying.

"You need to be young when you learn. We can't have you disbelieving. We can't have you thinking you know this world better than us. You understand?"

I am numb, but still manage to nod. The sun is too bright and the milk in my cereal is too cold, and Gramma has reverted to a version of herself that I tried so hard to forget but could never quite shake. The black water. The swaying. The melody. The blood.

"Eva, we can't help what we are born into. We can only accept it and do what we can to live as fully as possible. Are you following?"

Another nod. She is satisfied.

"This is something that has been passed down since your Great-Great-Great Grandma."

I stare blankly. She was dancing around her point. The swaying. The blood.

"The land we live on is old, Eva. And old lands, old waters, tend to hold things that are hard to understand. I'm going to tell you a story, Eva, and no matter what you think, you will have to do horrible, monstrous things because of it. It's not fair, but it's the way we live.

"A long time ago, your Great-Great-Great Grandma Carolina rose from the lake on our land. She was not a human being, rather a creature native to our lake. Let's call her a mermaid, Eva. You like mermaids, right?"

I think of my fairytale picture books. The mermaids have long, green hair and beautiful faces. "I like mermaids," I manage to say. The words almost choke in my throat, but I push them out.

"Your Great-Great-Great Grandma was from a dying breed. Only a handful of mermaids were left hiding in the deepest parts of the lake. You see, something new moved in there, something large and wicked. We call him Enoch.

"Enoch is hungry, and each year he must satisfy his hunger. He ate and ate and ate until your Great-Great-Great Grandma was the last of her kind. She was desperate, so she made a deal. In exchange for her life, she would give Enoch a life each year. He agreed, and she crawled from the lake."

I look down and notice my nails digging into my soft palm. I uncurl my hand, and half-moons blister red across it. "Eva, look me in the eyes when I'm talking to you," Gramma says, snapping me to attention. I shift in my seat and let my nails sink back into my skin.

"Carolina stayed on land so long that her tail cracked in two, giving her broken legs that grew calloused and numb to any pain. Story goes, she found a man. She must've, given that she had a daughter. The man was the first one fed to Enoch. He loved the taste of human men so much he demanded his annual sacrifice be a man. Now, each summer solstice, we bring Enoch a man. We sing the song of your Great-Great-Great Grandma's kind. We dance. We thank him. You're old enough, and tomorrow is the solstice. You will help from here on out. I'm old. I can't do this forever, and your Momma can't do this alone."

I sit shell-shocked at the table. I choose my words carefully. "What if…" I pause, "What if we just don't kill someone? Don't give Enoch anything at all, I mean."

"Then we die." Gramma's face is grim. "He will pull us from the land one by one, year by year, until nothing is left. That is the deal Carolina made, and it is the deal us daughters are born into."

I throw bloodied body parts into the lake for the first time at age ten. This is what daughters are born into. I hold hands with Momma and Gramma and sway as the dark waters gulp down the flesh. We hum the melody of our ancestor. I am slow to pick it up but get it in the end. When Gramma and Momma are finally asleep, I go back to the water's edge, still bloodied, my baby doll in hand, and throw it as far as I can into the nothingness.

I'm suspended underwater, unable to breathe. The sound of Gramma's humming fills up my ears with water. One by one, my limbs are slowly hacked from my body. The sound of my bones breaking apart fills my ears with water. I try to scream, but Momma places a blood-stained finger to my lips, still hacking off my remaining leg with her free hand. I watch as the black waters tinge red with my own blood. Something from far below the lake floor grabs hold of my limbs one by one. I am unable to fight as the tendrils curl around my torso and pull me down to the depths. It has had a taste of me and decided it wants more. I am ripped apart gently, reverently by the monster I have been tasked to keep at bay. Water fills my lungs, and I bite my tongue, remembering Momma shushing me, fearing the blood on her hand more than the teeth sinking half-moons into my flesh. I will not scream. Momma and Gramma watch and hum.

I am fifteen when I kill someone for the first time. Gramma is dying and wants to be sure I can do it. She's bed-ridden, but insists Momma carry her to the maimed body in the yard. Gramma looks so frail as she stares at the body. "You've done well, Eva," she says.

He lived a town over, we met while exploring the same nature trail, and his name was Aidan. He was sweet and called me pretty. I knew I'd kill him from the moment we locked eyes because I had no time for other options.

I asked him, "Do you want to go swimming at my family's lake?" and he immediately said yes in a smooth, southern accent. People go missing in the summer heat on trails all the time. We walked ten minutes to my home.

I stripped down to my bra and underwear and confidently waded shin deep into the lake despite never setting foot in it before. The water was warm and still. Each second I stood in the lake, I imagined Enoch reaching up to consume me.

Then Aidan stripped down to his boxers. He waded in next to me, gently held my face in his hands, and kissed me. My first kiss. His lips were soft. For a glorious moment, I let myself be a girl and pressed my forehead against his.

"Close your eyes and wait here a moment, I have a surprise for you," I whispered. If he noticed me shaking, he didn't bring it up.

"If the surprise is anything like how you kiss, I'll wait until the lake runs dry."

I made myself laugh. I waded to shore and grabbed the ax I'd stashed behind the big, old, moss-covered oak tree. *You don't have to do this*, I thought. *You can go back in the water, kiss him again, be young.* I looked back toward the house. Tall grasses blew softly in the wind, cradling the wooden frame. *Do you want to be responsible for Gramma dying? Mama? We are born killers, so what kind of killer are you?*

He never laid eyes on me again. He didn't even get to scream. The ax entered and exited his back, and his body broke. I dragged him to the grassy shore and chopped him into mangled pieces. Bones snapped as blood filled the air and coated my stomach, my legs, my face. Every inch of me that was skin turned red with Aidan.

I did well.

The flashes come even when I am numb to the action. My eyes shut and I am not twenty, I am four, and there is blood, swaying, a melody I can't make out in the humid summer air. Momma's getting weaker by the day. She never shook off the sight of Gramma's dead body despite the numerous lives she'd claimed. I hack an arm off with a hatchet, my eyes glazed over. Momma nods in approval from the porch, iced tea in her hand. I remember that night, the blood under her nails, and go further away into myself, the blood under my nails.

He's suspended underwater, unable to breathe. The sound of Gramma's humming fills up my ears with water. One by one, I slowly hack the limbs from his body. The sound of his bones breaking apart fills my ears with water. He tries to scream, but I place a blood-stained finger to his lips, still hacking off his remaining leg with my free hand. I watch as the black waters tinge red with his blood. One by one, Enoch grabs his limbs from far below the lake floor. He's unable to fight as the tendrils curl around his torso and pull him down to the depths. Momma and Gramma watch and hum. I stand apart from them and softly pick up the tune.

But tonight, Enoch is starving. First, he takes Gramma, then Momma, and all I can do is watch. I'm standing frozen as a doe stuck in headlights and don't fight when he comes for me. I never do. Enoch wraps his tendrils around my middle. As I'm pulled further and further down into the familiar grasp of my dreams, water sneaks into my lungs. I breathe a sigh of relief as his teeth bite half-moons into my middle.

Momma dies just before my thirtieth birthday. Summer is gone, and leaves fall in the soft autumn. She's buried in our family plot at the tiny church in our town. There are graves for each woman going back to my Great-Great-Great Grandma. Momma never understood why I didn't want a child of my own. This is just what daughters are born into. The swaying. The blood. The dark. *What kind of killer am I?*

I am thirty, it's the solstice, and I am alone with the memories of a child who didn't know what lay ahead. For the first time, the only body for Enoch is that of a daughter. Dusk has fallen, and I have made peace with the notion that Enoch can end my bloodline with me.

I wade ankle-deep into the waters for the first time since Aidan. Small pebbles dig into my feet. I wait. My mind has gone as placid as the lake itself. "Enoch will come and finish this," I whisper like a prayer, over and over again. As the night drags on, my eyes grow too heavy, and I fall asleep with my head nestled into the tall grasses, warm water waving over my body like a blanket. For once, the nightmare doesn't come.

I wake up at the first light of dawn. There is nothing. No Enoch. No monster. Just myself. The blood. The swaying. The dark waters catching the sunlight. There is no Enoch. There is no monster. I jolt up and run into the lake, water splashing in my wake. I wade in deeper. The swaying. The blood. Deeper still. The sticky air. The melody.

For the first time in my life, I allow myself to scream. Mama can't shush me from underground. I scream for my family, for the daughters, for Enoch to appear. My throat grows hoarse, my voice cracks to the point of fracturing, and still I scream and run further and further into the waters. My head submerges, and I continue screaming into the mass grave. The melody. Bloody hand in bloody hand. I never learned to swim and don't fight as I sink. I close my eyes, and I am four. I open them, and my rotted baby doll is within arm's reach. I am out of air and no longer scream. I extend my arm to the doll.

I am thirty/I am twenty/I am fifteen/I am ten.

I am four years old. I close my eyes and hear Momma whisper, "Go to bed, baby. You weren't supposed to know. Go to bed now, baby. Go to bed."

Pastorale

by Cormack Baldwin and EV Smith

It was supposed to be a perfect vacation. No, it was *going* to be a perfect vacation. Horatio had peered into every future he could see long enough to understand, and he had found rolling hills and whispering waves. For him, it would be a break from the city, with its fates and possibilities tangled into a single, pulsating knot. For Davide, a break from the bereaveds' requests for the passage of their troublesome loved ones. They would not be a minor seer and a psychopomp, but tourists. There would be sweet country air mixed with the salt tang of the ocean. There would be a seaside cottage painted in pastels.

"There's a body in the pipe organ," Davide informed Horatio matter-of-factly not ten minutes after they entered the stone cathedral, the first stop on their itinerary.

Perhaps it was his fault for bringing a psychopomp on vacation. The thought of skeletal remains sandwiched between oak and ivory made Horatio queasy. "They used to do that, I think. Churches and such."

Davide's lips pressed into a half frown as he walked over to the behemoth structure, so large it forced the pews to crowd together like teeth in a too-small mouth. "No, this is recent. They're not at peace at all."

Horatio swallowed. Flickers of darkest night entered the static of futures. He opened his mouth to ask a thousand questions at once. *Can you see them? Why would they be in the pipe organ, not the wall? How recent? Last century or last week? Do we have to do anything about it?*

He rubbed his eyes, forcing away charcoals and reds that crept like disembodied veins into his vision, as well as the dread swirling in his stomach. There were good futures yet. Shepherds with little yarn shops. Seaside toffee, the kind with chunks of salt. Nice things. Things that did not include bodies in instruments. "Is this something you'd like to focus on?"

He needn't have asked. Davide was already lifting away the outer panel of the pipe organ. Its designer evidently hadn't thought to install screws to protect entombed corpses.

"What are you doing?" Horatio protested as Davide leaned the panel against a wall.

"I'm a mortician, it's my duty," Davide replied.

"I'm a bookkeeper, that doesn't mean—" he began, but the words dried up in his throat. There, and in the firework of futures, was a body—fresh, rotting, leathery, skeletal, a thousand ways at a thousand points of discovery. White, at least for now, dark hair, younger than not. And very, very dead. "Oh, dear Lord."

"Mm," Davide agreed. He traced a finger down the body's unbuttoned dress shirt, clean of blood, before hooking a finger around the middle hem. Initially, Horatio thought he was just pulling the shirt aside. Instead, the cavity in the man's abdomen gaped back at him. Red slick glistened over the bump of vertebrae.

A suggestion to call the police was abandoned before he could even attempt it. The odds of anything good coming out of the authorities seeing a Black man and a Filipino man standing over a body after vandalizing a church were astronomically low. At least Davide assisted in murder investigations for his work, though usually at the behest of his partner, Richard.

No amount of rationalization would make him feel better. Bucolic futures fizzled and popped out of existence, consigned to pastel flickers in a world of stone and somber faces. And that was before Davide started speaking to the empty air.

"Ah, hello. My name is Davide." The mortician removed his hand from the man's empty abdomen and gestured a gore-streaked finger toward Horatio. "This is Horatio, a friend of mine." After a moment, Davide turned and said, "His name is Andrew Germeyer. He was an architect."

"Pleasure," Horatio lied. No, he oughtn't be rude. Not the man's fault he had been murdered. "I'm sorry about what happened to you."

For a moment, they waited in silence, then Davide shook his head. "I'm afraid he doesn't know what happened to him. The last thing he remembers is putting on the kettle at home." To the air, he said, "Even in non-traumatic deaths, the endings frequently aren't easily accessible. Nothing to worry about."

It seemed rational for one to worry about the fact that his guts resembled a poor man's wallet, and evidently, Andrew agreed.

"Would telling the minister help you move on?" Davide asked. Pause. "If you'd prefer to find out what happened, it may be more prudent to go to the police. Alternatively, I know a fine private detective—" A frown, perhaps at having the extolling of his boyfriend's virtues cut short. "Alright. Do you know where I might find him?"

It was not the manner in which Horatio had expected to take tea in a seaside cottage, but the minister's wife, Julia, was polite enough to provide it with a platter of biscuits. Horatio watched her throughout the futures, murmuring, crying, excusing herself to other rooms, as he took tentative sips. Knowing that it wasn't poisoned didn't make him feel better.

"Everyone loved Andrew," Julia said after Davide explained their visit. "He only moved here a few years ago, but he's really made himself at home."

"How wonderful," Horatio said.

"He died last night," Davide said. "Do you know of anything that could have been happening then?"

She considered it for a moment, then shook her head. "Well, I was home with the children. Gerald—my husband—was running a community meeting at the pub until nearly ten. Much of the town would have been there, I imagine. We're tight-knit here."

Dozens of faces ticked by in the back of Horatio's mind, each giving the same alibi. Everyone had seen each other, and none of them had done it. He nodded, and Davide gave a short sigh.

"Would anyone else have access to the cathedral?" Davide asked.

Julia shook her head, eyes trained on the floor.

Horatio drowned his burgeoning headache with a swallow of tea. This wasn't going anywhere, not that he could see. Future alibis paraded by his vision, each as steady as the last. "Well, we would hate to keep you, ma'am. Thank you for your hospitality. Would it be possible for us to speak to your husband?"

She worried the hem of her shirt as possible versions of her stammered apologies, or ushered them out the door. "Well, he'll be at the church today, and probably won't be home until evening."

Davide perked up at that, and the babble of voices cleared like a radio being tuned through static. A chorus of tips, threats, and excuses. A hundred faces, suspicious and welcoming in turn. A future of interviews in between slammed doors. People talking, talking, saying—

"*Well, I was at the town meeting, anyone could tell you that.*"

"Who the hell are you? Don't look like any constables I've ever seen. Get the hell out before I—"

"One step more and I shoot. Try me! Try—"

—Nothing he wanted to hear. "Thank you," he interrupted before Davide could speak, "but I'm sure we can find it if we need to. We only came because we thought the minister ought to know."

Her frown deepened, but she accepted effusive thanks for the hospitality and walked them both to the door.

It was not a triumphant return to the hotel, though Horatio had assured Davide that it was an opportunity to strategize and not just a rest for his headache. He'd explained what he'd seen from the futures where they asked around, leaving out the death threats.

"Nothing of use," Davide sighed. "You said they'll all have alibis?"

Horatio nodded. It was mostly true. Everyone gave alibis, but everyone also confessed. If there were a killer among them (and he had it on good evidence that one did not lose their organs by accident), they wouldn't confess any more easily than someone bullied into making it up. "This may be beyond our skillset," he said.

Somewhere, in some future, the shutters kept flapping open and shut on a deathly, dry wind. As Horatio peered into that orange haze, Davide announced, "I'm going to call Richard."

The futures scrambled to keep up with this decision, sparking randomly between shores, fields, and returns to the city, and dry air, dead earth, and mocking clouds.

"I don't think that's—" he started, but the words seemed to stick in his throat. The static of the future washed over his vision like a television whose antennas had been knocked askew. Blacks, reds, oranges, empty whites. Screams, sighs of wind, nothing at all.

Richard's voice, tinny from the connection, cut through the wall of sheer improbability. Davide must have already called. Hadn't it only been a second? Time wasn't acting right, it—

Desolate air burning sun, everything is dry, dry, dry, fire on the–

Vortex of clouds, clockwise clockwise switch turn turn and churn and–

"Are you sure—" static turned Richard's voice to a mumble. A cough cleared it again. "Well, if I were you, I would look into the minister. He's the hinge in the alibis, isn't he?"

"Oh, good point, love. He wasn't available earlier, but—"

It's all falling it's all falling it's all falling–

A hand on his shoulder. "Are you alright?" Davide's voice was an anchor in a stormy sea.

Here was where a Poirot, a Sherlock, someone other than a bookkeeper with a tendency toward prophecy, would say something to set the whole timeline right. Phosphenes of lush green and turquoise meant it wasn't a given, not yet. He could unwind the machine and pull out the key, let Davide give up so naturally he wouldn't even notice. The best Horatio managed was, "I need air."

"Of course," said Davide. "We can go down to the shore for a bit, how about that? After that, Richard suggested going back to the church."

Horatio mentally threw out the last sentence. The thought of the gentle roll of waves soothed his burning mind. He nodded.

The sky flickered between blues and blacks, reds and yellows as they walked. Horatio squeezed his eyes shut to keep the shifting ground from tricking him into tripping, but–

Broken promise, broken bones, break the city, broken tome–

–the smell of the ocean was what caught him first, the tang of salt mixed with the rich scent of decay. A breeze played across his face, depositing grit that wouldn't come out without many showers. Slowly, he opened one eye, then the other.

Teal water lapped at the sand, rolling tiny, white stones into oblivion. Even in his doubled, tripled vision, a single boat bobbed peacefully along in the placid water. Through the window, he could make out moving shapes. Fishermen, or, or—

Red sky in morning, black clouds bring no rain. Run from what has waited on the shore, not sleeping, not fearing. Run, for the deal is broken.

Breathe in the musk of rot, the only thing that will be left of you when it is done. Gaping silver faces, eyes twitching awake as white mold turns scales to fur.

Look ahead, see what the vengeful sea has offered. Colossus in yielding flesh. Its tentacles reach far into the horizon. The squid roils with death. Darkened veins paint its endless arms. It hits you, that smell, that awful smell, not its death alone—

Horatio dropped to his knees and vomited. The hungry sand drank the bile all at once or perhaps not at all or perhaps never again because—

It's coming it's coming it's coming it's—

The brief peace of unconsciousness was interrupted by his senses coming on one by one, as if each had to be checked before continuing. Vision: speckles of red sky and falling fish, but mostly a tin ceiling that swung back and forth. Smell: salty, but not infernal. Taste: rancid.

Hearing… he wasn't sure. The futures had retreated, only babbling in the background. But he couldn't make out a single word of the overlapping voices of the present. Maybe he'd suffered some sort of brain damage, and that was why he'd fainted. Just his luck.

"*Nagising siya, saglit lang.* How are you feeling?" Davide's voice. His face, surrounded by echoes of the future, appeared above him.

Horatio blinked up at him, as well as the repeated versions of him. "Where am I?" he asked.

Another face, sea-worn and curious, entered his vision.

"Fishing boat. These ladies saw you and offered to help. Horatio, this is Celeste, Tess, and Rosa." Davide pointed at each, though only Tess was visible to wave. "Aunties, this is Horatio, as I said."

"One too many?" Tess asked. The aunties behind her chuckled, and she cut them a glare.

"No, we were... we were going to..." the memories kept slipping away. He wasn't making his denial sound more plausible. "We were going to the bait shop?" That felt right. It stood in the future, hooks and leads rusted, beaten by the unforgiving sun.

"The Bait and Tackle?" one of the aunties, perhaps Celeste (somewhere in the clang of futures, that name appended itself to her), chimed in. "That place is fantastic. Gives us free bait when they have extra. Nothing much, just some chum each summer to welcome us back, but better than buying it, eh?"

Pink and red wriggled across Horatio's vision. He couldn't recognize anything from the flashes, but the mixed dread and nausea told him that it was something important. Bracing himself, he asked, "Do you have some now?"

Celeste scrutinized him, clearly wondering what sort of man woke up from a bender to ask about fishing. "Just got it yesterday. You'll need to pay if you want any, though. Here," she shuffled out of sight, then returned with a cooler as large as her torso. With a flourish, she lifted the lid.

Fish Gather to Listen

Had anything been left in Horatio's stomach, it certainly would have come up. The smell, gamey and rank, filled the microscopic cabin as a wave of red skies filled Horatio's vision. Even unflappable Davide gave a short, "Hm," at the sight of the off-pink paste, slippery chunks of intestine surfacing like fish. On top, like a garnish, lay a heart the size of a fist.

Horatio slid off the bed, catching himself on the railing. "I'm sorry, do you mind if I talk to my friend alone for a moment?" he asked.

"You can go to the deck," Rosa said.

"Thank you." Horatio ran his hand along the wall until he reached the door, then shouldered it open.

Davide had to duck to make it through. After easing it shut behind him, he turned back to Horatio. "Well, either the Bait and Tackle doesn't know, or they're in on it as well."

Sealed storm shutters flaking paint and rusted iron bolts snapped shut–the thud of Davide's solid body on a steel door that won't budge– "By the time that we get there, the shop will be closed," he warned. "What do you suppose we do now?"

Davide's somber expression and silver hair matched the gray sea around them, the crests of sloshing white. "I'm a mortician. I need to return what's left to Andrew."

And so, with Davide fifty pence lighter, Horatio found himself holding an ice chest on the threshold of a pipe organ.

"—it's not much, but hopefully you'll feel more whole," Davide was explaining to the air.

Horatio turned his back. Even then, there was no escape from the slick sound of blood, flashes of red streaking Davide's fingers.

The noise's abrupt stop was not the relief it should have been. "That's interesting," Davide said slowly. "How do you suppose this got here?"

Horatio could neither offer nor hear a response.

"What did you find?" Horatio asked as they walked back to the hotel. A light rain had started up, interspersed with flashes of deep, viscous red. He didn't really want to know.

Davide ignored the question. "He remembered something. He told me that the day before he was taken from this world, the good minister came to visit him," he explained, "to convince him not to attend the next community meeting. He would be the only one not in attendance."

Carnage solidified in the writhing futures. Horatio could see it now, the two of them marched at gunpoint past the rivers of fish, a mob of villagers at their back. "Everyone is in on it, then," Horatio said. A laugh bubbled out of his throat as the realization hit him along with a rain of rotting fish in his nostrils and the corners of his vision. "What, are we going to get the whole town arrested? Or, do you want to be the one in that cooler?"

"They can't kill me, you're the only one who really needs to be concerned," Davide said.

Horatio slapped a hand to his face, the sting briefly chasing away the encroaching desolation. "Oh, even better! Is that why you won't let what needs to be, be?"

"It's what's right," Davide said.

Horatio's blood threatened to boil over. "'What's right' is going to get us killed! Oh, I'm sorry, it's going to get *me* killed, I'll not rope you into this." He hated himself for the hurt on Davide's face. He hated himself for being here. He hated that somewhere in there, he still wanted to grasp for something beautiful, and hold it tight. A turquoise sea, an ice cream melting onto white sand. Tears threatened to spill over his cheeks and join the sea. "Davide, I brought you along because I thought we could both use a break. A week with no more death, no more calamity."

Davide bit his lip, eyes scanning the horizon of bobbing boats and open ocean. He watched a lemon-yellow trawler putter into the setting sun as Horatio watched a future where it sank. "There's no getting away," Davide said finally, certainty exchanged for resignation. "I realize that this isn't what you wanted, but this is what we do. People die everywhere. The future goes on everywhere. We make the best of what we can't control."

The boat rose again, pulled by a phantom hook, waiting for something that had never happened.

It was dark when the minister, an aging man with a hangdog expression Horatio suspected was permanent, came to where they waited on the whitewashed porch. The comforting hum of charming, consistent life in the little town had sputtered and suffocated into a quiet that unnerved Horatio more than any storm.

"And how can I help you boys?" came his weary baritone, as he eyed Horatio carefully. Horatio tried to make himself smaller, never mind that he was nearly thirty-two years old.

Davide gave a tight smile. "I'm sorry to interrupt your evening. I spoke to your wife earlier."

"Ah, yes. Thank you for alerting me to the... situation. It's a terrible business, Lord help us." The minister bowed his head in respect.

"I just have a few questions, if that'd be alright," Davide pushed. He didn't give the minister a chance to refuse. "There was a community meeting last night?"

The minister cleared his throat with more force than necessary. "Well, yes. It ran late. Lots of business to address, you know. New construction."

Davide narrowed his eyes. "Without your architect? Perhaps you came by his house. Told him to stay home."

The Minister schooled his terror behind an awkward smile that made no attempt to reach his eyes. "I'm sorry?"

"And perhaps you came back from the meeting, with all the people in town lying on your behalf. Perhaps you killed Andrew, and shoved him somewhere no one but you would have reason to access for a while," Davide continued, ignorant of or disinterested in how Horatio's stomach dropped further with every syllable.

The minister sputtered then straightened, anger replacing his fear. "Now you listen here, you filthy—"

Davide held up his hand, and the minister stopped dead. "I don't actually need you to tell me why I found this on the body. In fact, you may want to save that speech for the authorities." In his palm, Davide clutched a black scrap from the priest's chasuble. The low light made him look like the corpses he swore to serve. "I just need to know who exactly did it, and why. Why was there a man in the pipe organ, diced up to be dumped into the sea?"

The minister withered, giving a small cough. "Not dumped," he replied primly. "Given. The ritual requires entrails to be sacrificed into the water. The organ was just a convenient place to store him away from scavengers until the tides wouldn't carry the corpse into trawler nets."

Horatio blinked. "The ritual?" Images of hands raised in worship clicked into place.

"Our town serves the ocean," the minister said. "It has for centuries, if not longer. Each year we find someone who does not know its glory, and we give them as a gift. You must understand, we do what we must to receive its blessing—if we don't—" His voice broke, the last of his resolve shattering into terror. "Without the seas, no one comes. Without fish, we cannot eat. Either they die or we all do." He turned imploringly to Horatio, tears streaking down his cheeks.

Horatio hesitated. Through the swarm of rot and desolation, he could still do the math. No easy answer anywhere in the crashing wave of reality. There was no killing it or sating it. One person a year, ad infinitum. Or the town, the county, expanding out and out and—

He bit back the wave of futures. Reluctantly, he nodded. "The ritual is what's holding it back, whatever it is." If there were a solution, it wouldn't show itself any time soon. One did not argue with elder gods.

"You give them no rites," Davide snapped.

"Their rite is to honor our god," the minister ground out.

"You've taken their life. You have no right to their afterlife as well. We have enough evidence to—"

Let it break, let it grow, let it come from the sea. Years of placation will never make up for an eternity of want. The contract is broken, the deal is—

"How about a compromise?" Horatio suggested. The others stared. He continued as if his voice wasn't shaking. "Your town knows about what they're holding back, correct?"

The minister paused, but eventually agreed, "They're aware. They do their duty to help each year."

"Then sacrifice one of them, someone who knows what's coming and will want to save the people they care about." The words turned to ash in his mouth as green and blue spread across the futures. "Offer them the rites they deserve. Let them move on. If you can promise that, we'll leave on the first train tomorrow morning." He looked between the two. "Do we have a deal?"

Horatio wished he could take comfort watching fields of snowy white sheep roll by train windows.

Davide had almost said the words so many times that they felt familiar by the time he finally asked, "Did we even do anything?"

Somewhere, never far enough away, there remained a town that would slit someone else's belly next year. In another year's time they would gut another, organs spilling out in halos before being fed to the gulls. Burials, cremation, funerals: it didn't change that moment when someone went from an end to a means.

But the red had receded. Veins of annihilation no longer crept into visions of family asking how his vacation went. As pastel pastorals passed by, Horatio said, "No, I don't think we did."

Sealskins, Daughters, Teeth

by Malda Marlys

A lonely fisherman spots one of the seal-women on the beach, takes his admiration for love, or because he revels in the taking. He hides her skin. She keeps his house and bears his brats. One day she reclaims her stolen self and disappears into the sea. The epilogue promises generations of lucky fishermen, but doesn't linger on the ones left ashore.

Some of us must stretch our bellies in the wet sand, raise those slightly uncanny children, and live and die on a fog-soaked beach that stinks of rancid fish, or where would the stories come from?

I used to seethe at my father's folk, huffing my inhuman growls as they walked by. They who dreamed their best and most daring dreams of slightly better boats and trawled the seas for fish that rightly belong to my people. I have better uses for my spleen in my old age, but I miss that certainty. They're as fit for their own world as the seals are.

And I? I have no people. I have half-things for sisters—I am a half-thing—and a mother who left us to our fate.

My father was a good soul. He didn't keep his seal-wife against her will. She gave him the skin and told the tale with clear, soft eyes. I cast her as silly and thoughtless in the sour little lies I spun myself to explain our abandonment. Easier to detest her that way.

Whatever her motives, Father fancied himself a poet and a dreamer and too good for the girls in town.

I may have inherited that streak from him, come to think.

He didn't know his children would be something more like seals than not, something terribly unlike seals in every way, wretched. I like to think he'd never have sired us if he had.

The teeth usually come out right, and that's worse. Just try not to bite your own tongue off with shearing teeth and no proper snout.

Misery is a spine that means to twist its way through deep water and has no freedom in its ribcage. Shame is hide as fragile as seaweed, and it burns before you know what shame is.

Father's long dead. Before his time, it was, his poet's will worn out by the slow trickle of wife and daughter after daughter slipping away with the seafoam.

I think one of my sisters ate him, but that's her affair. He wouldn't have minded.

Mother lingered ashore seven years before she threw herself back into the salt. And seven little ones she left behind. Might have been no malice in it at all. Seal pups are ready to face the world alone earlier than human whelps. So, she left us. Left me, the eldest, to manage all the rest.

Left us here in the sand where the sea goes to rot.

I might wring her perfect neck if I found her again. It wouldn't do the others any good, only make me feel better, but nothing else ever has.

Selkie-spawned girls try to go home, you see. We can't understand that we're as useless in the waves as the dolts around us.

There I am again, wanting a story where I'm sinned against, not a grim mistake. Seal pups, not too clever for their own good, know they can't swim. Us? We'll drown given half a chance. Two of my sisters went that way young, and we all tried. It was always me or Father when anyone managed to drag us back.

Six sisters went before me.

The two drowned children, and a third years later with full knowledge of what lay between her and the sea.

The one who followed her teeth. Don't know where she disappeared to, but I hope she's happy in her hunger.

One turned sailor, and the ship went down with all hands. Perhaps that was what became of our mother. Sheer wanderlust and a misadventure that kept her from an intended return. That's a sweeter story, and I mistrust the taste, but it could be.

The last and best of us had the will for a life on the rocks. She took a husband.

She chose poorly.

He wasn't like our father, and when he saw her smile at the sea like she never would at him one time too many, he took her from me.

I didn't eat him. Not because I wasn't tempted, but because he didn't deserve it. I've lived a long time as a fisherwoman. I know how to work neatly around bone. All the quiet creeping things of the sea may eat him at their leisure.

Tempting to think of him as a sacrifice, but who'd want the bastard? More likely what made that night of quiet butchery different was knowing I'd lost my littlest sister, my last, failed charge.

Or it could have simply been time. I was the first and the worst of my mother's pups. The vast cold of the sea coaxes great size from its denizens, but oh, so slowly. Maybe my seven sevens of years on land were a sort of infancy.

When I tossed that last, lonely fillet of fisherman to the waves, I followed it. I thought I'd be the fifth sister to drown, that the sea would have me at last, and good riddance.

But the cold wouldn't enter my bones. My skirts floated, and then they tore, and then they were too small to regard. The tail I always should have had sliced through the water, and a snout long enough for all my wonderful wealth of teeth parted the darkness. I dove deeper than the sea ever was so close to the island.

A lonely fisherman takes a sealwife, and she is sloe eyed and graceful and good, and she leaves him bereft when her work is done, a mother of monsters whose daughters may forgive her when they grow up at last.

Daughter of the Sea

by Hope Elizabeth Kidd

I can see the headlines now:

June 3, 1989 / Woman Gives Birth to Freak of Nature! or *Woman Gives Birth to Mermaid!*

No. No one must ever know about her.

I'm perched on top of the toilet lid, staring at my daughter in the bathtub. At least, I think she's my daughter. I see no genitals, but her baby face looks girlish to me. I've already named her: Cordelia – "daughter of the sea." I had named her before she was born, before she came out like this. Cordelia was my great grandmother's name. Strange, bizarre that my baby's name fits her so perfectly.

Three flaps of skin on her neck softly open and close. When they open, I see burgundy-colored flesh underneath, deep flesh that makes my skin crawl. Below a chubby belly with no belly button, her skin stops, and scales begin: silvery, almost glistening. Six inches of scales that fan into tail fins streaked with cyan. Her closed eyes are lined with dark lashes, and dark hair covers her head.

She's beautiful. Disconcerting and impossible, but beautiful. But what would the rest of the world say about her? That she's a monster?

Adrian is due home in a week. What will he say? I don't have a way to reach him on the oil rig; I'll have to show him this creature, our daughter. I wonder if he will accuse me of infidelity. The baby cannot be his after all. But I haven't slept with anyone else, human *or* mythical creature. I myself didn't believe in merpeople until my own daughter emerged from my body, smelling of brackish water.

I went into labor early. We don't know the neighbors yet, don't know their phone numbers, and they're too far away to walk to for help. Except one woman: Elsie, our closest neighbor, an older, retired woman. She was the first person to come over when we moved to Sagwon, Alaska a month ago. She's our closest neighbor, though her house is a quarter of a mile away.

If I had given birth in the hospital, I wouldn't be sitting here right now, gazing at my sleeping daughter. She would be in a research lab under fluorescent lights. A nurse would have screamed as she came out, and the doctor would have said, "My god, what *is* this?" and everyone would have crowded around. They wouldn't have let me hold her. They would have whisked her away, and the FBI would have come to my hospital bed.

As it is, I gave birth to her in the bathtub two hours ago, with Elsie as stand-in midwife. She came over as soon as I called her, and she said we shouldn't radio for help. No,

I was too close, and she would help me give birth right here in the house. It would be perfectly fine.

Now, Elsie steps into the bathroom and places a hand on my shoulder. "I finished cleaning everything up. You should go lie down."

I look into her face, her wrinkles deep and friendly. "But I can't leave her here."

"She'll let you know when she's hungry again," nods Elsie.

She's right. When Cordelia was first born, she cried, breathing air.

Elsie had cleaned her, not gasping in shock at the silver-blue tail, not knitting her brows in confusion. Instead, I was the one gasping, screaming, panicking at the sight of her. Elsie had only said, "Oh!" and then "Look at that!" as if this were a surprise but not altogether unexpected.

As if we were the closest of friends, she had helped the baby latch onto a nipple. She had calmed me while Cordie sucked, and I cried. She drained the bloody water from the tub, helped me deliver the placenta, held ice packs on my perineum. She refilled the tub with warm water as my daughter and I lay there. I watched as Cordelia breathed through her nose as she nursed, the gills on her neck firmly closed.

Now, I feel an animalistic love for her, but I'm still weeping. "I don't understand. I don't understand," I keep saying as Elsie helps me into a nightgown, assists with underwear and a giant pad for the bleeding. She takes me to my bed. "I don't understand," I say again, but she shushes me, and I've barely closed my eyes before sleep takes over.

Elsie knocks on my door mid-morning. I'm so grateful to see another human being, I embrace her even though I hardly know her. Then again, she just helped me deliver a baby mermaid; she's heard my guttural screams and grunts; she's seen ... everything.

"Coffee?" I offer. "Tea?"

"Coffee, love," she says. "How was the night?"

I tell her that for a while Cordie slept in my bed with me. She was fine out of the water for three full hours, but then her tail became dry and sticky. I hand Elsie a mug of coffee and motion to the sugar and milk on the countertop.

"How did you know?" I blurt. "And why didn't it scare you the fuck away? Have you ... seen this before? How is this even possible? I'm not dreaming, right? Is this really happening?"

She smiles, in that way that's both unnerving and comforting. But she says nothing.

"Elsie?" I prompt. "*What's happening*?"

"Come with me," she says, leading the way to the bathroom. She sits in front of the bathtub, on the cold tile floor, and motions for me to sit next to her.

"She's beautiful," Elsie says, nodding at Cordie, asleep in the clear water. She turns to me. "This *is* really happening. It's no dream." She pauses. "Have you ever heard of the Marris?"

I shake my head.

"There's a legend my grandmother used to tell me, though my mother thought it was hogwash. About the sea people."

"Sea people?"

"Yes, half-human, half-fish. My grandmother saw a Marris once. She lived several hundred miles south of here, though. She was a child, out on the water with her father, and saw one. One that followed near the boat and allowed my grandmother to see it, but not her father. She spent the rest of her years trying to prove their existence. In her research, she found near thirty claims of Marris sightings in Alaska alone."

"In cold water? In the Arctic?" All my visions of mermaids swimming in warm seas in sparkling sunshine shatter like glass.

"Yes," nods Elsie. "Anyway, she told me that they don't like us, though sometimes they allow a human who has seen them to live. Other times, they kill those who have seen."

Questions swirl in my head: How did the Marris come into existence? How can this possibly be real? How do they breathe in the air *and* in water? And most importantly, how did *I* become pregnant with one? I only ask her the last question.

She smiles. "Ah, you see, they have a way of ... orchestrating circumstances."

"What do you mean?"

"Well, they can't procreate like you and I. So they have to ... make things happen. Think about it. You're living out in the middle of nowhere. What brought you to rural Alaska?"

"Adrian's job," I shrug.

"But he could work on a rig in any other place. What brought you to the rig *here*?"

I realize I don't really know. Adrian told me he was offered a good job working in oil, but it would require a move to a rural area in a frigid climate. I said okay. I didn't care as long as I was with him, and I could take a few years off work to raise our baby.

"But," I say, "are you saying *they* made him get this job?"

"I can't say for sure what they're capable of. I just know they have great power." She pauses. "Think some more. Did you ever see her shape in a sonogram?"

"No," I said. "Well, I had one early on. At ten weeks. The technician said she couldn't get a good view of the lower body. She said to come back. Then Adrian's job ended, and so did the insurance. When he started the new job, well, I was so close to the due date, I didn't see a point."

"Mm hmm," nods Elsie. "And do you have family? Or friends who know you were pregnant and will be checking up on you, wanting you to send them pictures?"

I shake my head. "No. My parents have passed, and I'm an only child. And Adrian is estranged from his family, except for a sister. And you're the only person I know here."

"Exactly," Elsie nods again. "And finally, think about why you and Adrian moved into the house closest to mine when I'm the only person around who believes in the Marris?"

For a moment, I can't speak. It's all too much. "But why *me*?" I demand. "Why would they choose *me*?"

"I don't know," answers Elsie. "I don't know that we'll ever know."

When Adrian came back, he threw his arms around me before realizing my belly was empty. I showed him Cordelia, and he started with "What the hell is *that*?", left to go for a walk, came back, screamed at me and slammed his fist on the table, went outside again, came back again. But by that evening, he was holding her, teary-eyed, as he kissed her cheeks and caressed her head. I explained everything that Elsie had told me, and he said, "It's the goddamn strangest thing, and I don't understand, but she's here, and she's ours." And later, shaking his head, he added, "Yeah, no one can know about her."

But now, I am so sad for my daughter. Cordelia is fourteen months old, and she has lived most of her life in the bathtub. She tries to swim back and forth but becomes frustrated with the mere four feet of length. The rest of the time, she's sleeping in our bed with me, or spending a brief amount of time in the living room. She can't sit up to play with toys, but sometimes I hold her in my lap and read her books, her tiny fingers reaching out to touch the puppy on the page. She eats solid food, but not much. I can hardly find any food she likes. She eats fish and canned peas, the occasional noodle. She still receives most of her nutrition from my breastmilk. Obviously, she's never been seen by a doctor, but I can tell she isn't growing well. I know that it's the confined space, not being in her natural habitat, not being with other beings like her, the lack of ocean food. When Adrian's on the rig for weeks at a time, it's horribly lonely here, just Cordie and me, although Elsie comes to visit sometimes.

One night, Cordie is fussy, and I can't calm her. She isn't happy in the bathtub, she won't go to sleep, won't be rocked or snuggled. I look at Adrian, who's taking a turn with her.

"What are we going to *do*?" I say. But somehow, we both know that what I mean is, "I think it's time to let her go."

Adrian's eyes fall, and he can't look at me or even at Cordie. He turns his head, placing his cheek against her hair. "We can't," he says.

"We *have* to," I answer over Cordie's squawks.

There is the longest pause as Adrian sways with her, and she finally quiets down. He looks back at me and says, "I know."

Fish Gather to Listen

We decide nighttime is best. Adrian has a friend with a motorboat. He just has to ask to borrow the keys. It's more than an hour's drive to Prudhoe Bay, but for the summer, the boat is parked in Sagwon River. Adrian stops the truck and helps Cordie and me out. August winds whip my hair. He assists us into the boat, and I almost fall, trying to hold the baby and balance. I zip a life jacket over my clothes as we start off. I'm afraid of being seen because it's light out, but he reminds me that everyone is fast asleep; it's past midnight. He drives the boat up the river to the bay, fighting choppy waters as I hold Cordie to my chest. Over the past few months, she's been able to spend less and less time out of the water, and she's starting to dry out. Her tail feels sticky.

Which only confirms that we are doing the right thing. But I don't know how it's going to work. Elsie assured me that the Marris will find her quickly because they'll know when one of their own is in their waters. But I don't know when the Marris will find her, and I don't know if she can fend for herself in an ocean. I worry about seals mistaking her for prey. I worry about how she will find food.

Cordelia's wide awake, babbling "wa wa" because she knows we're on the water. Her tail flops up and down. "Mama. Wa wa."

"That's right. You and Mama are on the water." I almost choke on tears as I say it.

We make it over the surf and out into the bay. Adrian says fifteen minutes out is far enough. The motor hums, and I close my eyes. Finally, Adrian stops the boat. "I think this is good," he says, looking back toward the land. It looks purple in the twilight.

I hold Cordelia under her arms and gaze into her chocolate eyes. "I love you *so much*," I say. "You're my sweet baby girl, and I love you." I nuzzle her neck with kisses until she giggles.

Adrian gathers us into a circle of three. He whispers into Cordie's ear, "I love you, I love you, I love you."

"Ma ma, Da da," she says. "Wa wa?" She points to the water.

"Yes," I say. "You're going to be so happy in the water." But I have no idea if this is true.

We decided that we can't just drop her in the water and go. Elsie is positive the Marris will come, and we decided to wait in the water until they do. Adrian holds Cordie while I strip naked then buckle the life vest back on. I jump into the ocean. Its cold lashes my skin and stops my heart for a moment. I can hardly breathe. "So cold," I manage, reaching my arms up for Cordie.

Adrian climbs down the ladder with her in one arm. He keeps hold of the lowest rung. "Holy shit," he stammers. "Freezing."

But Cordie laughs and splashes in my arms, her tail going wild. "Wa wa! Wa wa!"

I look around. "Okay, this is it." I turn away from the boat and scream as loudly as I can, "Come get your baby!" I pause "Are you coming? Come. Get. Your. Baby!"

Cordie wiggles in my arms. We let her swim back and forth between the two of us, and I try to control my spinning thoughts. What we are doing seems insane; maybe we *are* insane. I'm terrified that the Marris won't come, and I'm terrified they will. What was it Elsie said about them killing? My heart pounds harder and faster. But bigger than my dread and fear is the agonizing thought that my baby will soon be gone.

We wait for what seems like ages. My shivering is almost convulsing. I scream into the sky again: "Hey! Come get your baby! Come on!" Adrian yells, too. But maybe they can't hear us in the air. I take a deep breath, put my head under the water, and scream, "Come get your baby!" but it only sounds like gurgles.

I come up for a breath, go under again. I scream the command once more, then open my eyes for the briefest of seconds. Salt water stings my eyes, but what I see is horrifying. In the darkening, murky-blue water, a foot away from my face, I see another face. It's silvery with massive, sunken eyes on either side of its head like a fish. The eyes are empty pools, swirls of black. Sharp, scalloped gills protrude from both sides of its neck. Instead of hair, seaweed and kelp frame its face. Where a nose would be, there is flat, smoky skin with two nostrils. Its body curves into an absurdly long, gray tail, ending in sharp tail fins.

It opens its mouth and lets out a high-pitched shriek that stabs my ears. When its mouth opens, a thick, red liquid emerges and swirls into the ocean water. Its teeth are inch-long, narrow spikes. Its webbed hands reach toward me, but instead of fingers, it has five curved claws.

All this happens in an instant, and I know without a doubt that I am looking into the face of a Marris. But its grotesqueness, its hideousness, is unspeakable. It looks nothing like my beautiful baby. I come up gasping and screaming, scrambling in the water toward Adrian. In another second, I see my baby's face, and she has changed. She suddenly looks as repulsive as the thing I saw under the water: sunken, black-hole eyes; silver lips; sharp, protruding gills.

Did she always look like that and I couldn't see it, or did the water change her?

As I scramble toward Adrian, I manage "Adrian, they're h—" but I'm yanked under the water, something grasping my ankle and pulling me deep enough for the pressure to throb in my ears. I kick as hard as I can; it lets go, and, with my life jacket, I quickly bob back up to the surface. I glance around. I'm yards away from Adrian now. He's calling for me, and I swim toward him. He's not holding Cordelia.

"Where is she?" I demand. "Where is she?"

"She swam to them. They took her," he shakes his head. "Quick, get back on the boat." He thrusts me toward the ladder and pushes me up. Before I can get one foot on the bottom rung, Adrian screams behind me, and there's thrashing in the water. "Adrian!" I bellow. I'm terrified and keep climbing, but I slip and fall.

When I plunge under the water, a sudden, deep calm falls over the ocean and me. It is deathly quiet. Even the waves have stopped moving. I'm under the surface. I open my eyes, and I can see far into the blue. The first thing I see is Adrian a few yards away, already dead, bloody water swirling around him. The second thing I see is Cordelia, beautiful and grotesque at the same time, smiling at me. Her mouth opens and no words come out, but I can hear her voice inside my head: "Ma ma, bye bye." Then she turns and darts away into the blue. And the third thing I see is two of *their* hideous bodies swimming toward me, death in their eyes, and I don't have time to do anything else. In my head, I hear the words, "We have to do this," and then everything turns dark.

Itself

by Jan M. Flynn

It took up residence under the bridge not long after clawing its way out of its mother, who did her best to eat it, as she had the rest of the litter. Being the quickest, it sank its fangs into the nape of her neck and waited until her thrashing stopped.

It fed on her body until its shell hardened.

Moving downstream, it subsisted on fish and eels before it learned to extend its sinuous front limbs, the ones with the eyed claws, out of the water. When it snatched a sleepy muskrat one still-dark morning, it discovered its taste for warm blood. Prowling the shoreline at dusk and dawn, it kept its claws motionless until a young deer or an unguarded goat drew near.

With each feeding its strength increased. Its body swelled, filling out the tough scales that enclosed it until it grew itchy and tight and hot. Rubbing against stones on the river bottom, it felt its surface splitting in places, exposing its spongy interior. By now it had found its way to the grotto under the town bridge, drawn there by the downward-drifting smells of animal blood and human sweat. Wedging its soft body into the space, it drifted into a state halfway between life and death as the water around it cooled and thickened into ice.

In spring, it awoke to the reborn river water lapping against its new, tough casing. A breeze teased its nostrils with scents of flesh, arousing in it an urgent hunger. It stretched, its body much longer now, its powerful tails scooping space for itself in the gravelly bottom of the grotto. Above, there was movement and sound, although the sun was still below the horizon. Voices rose to a bellow above the din, utterances it instinctively deciphered and found surprisingly easy to reproduce.

Up on the bridge, a drover bellowed insults at the pig farmer whose herd surrounded his wagon. The farmer's reply, a marvel of obscene concision, allowed it to calibrate his position. It held its two front limbs just out of the water to sight its mark, and with a sudden snakelike motion, reached up and over both sides of the bridge at once. In a flash, it held a writhing pig in one claw and the farmer in another. The eyes in its claws surveyed the scene.

For a heartbeat, people and animals froze as they regarded the pig and the man hovering above them. Then the arms holding the victims whipped beneath the river's surface, and bedlam broke out on the bridge.

Underneath, it considered using its new ability to utter a threat, but there seemed little need, especially as its meal took up most of its attention. The young pig was succulent. The farmer was tougher, with stringy tendons and curdled fat, yet the taste of human was uniquely satisfying. It understood that it had found its proper food.

It stretched its tails and sucked on the farmer's remaining femur, listening. From above came a muffled cacophony: alarm bells, shouted orders, running feet. The noise was a fitting backdrop for thoughtful digestion. Settling back, it entertained itself by silently practicing human speech as the sun climbed above the eastern hills and cast its sparkling light on the water.

A different sort of sound, rhythmic knocking and banging, awoke it some days later. It wasn't hungry yet, but as soon as the afternoon light dimmed toward dusk, it sent up its front limbs, their luminous eyes investigating. The claws probed along a hastily erected wooden barrier arising on both sides of the bridge. It heard a staccato rush of feet toward the town gate, the ping of dropped hammers amid cries of terror, and one hoarse voice rising from the middle of the span.

"Take courage, men! Those cursed serpents can't break through our stout oak timbers!"

It raised its great, hooked beak above the water line and uttered a roar that buckled the knees of everyone on the bridge. Its limbs switched from exploring to smashing as it sent up more arms. Within moments, the oaken barrier was reduced to splinters which bobbed uselessly downstream. Tracking its challenger as the man ran headlong toward the gate, one of its claws plucked him off the cobblestones and waved him in the air in front of the walls as he screeched and babbled. Another claw, reaching from the opposite side, deftly twisted off the man's head, splattering the guards along the top of the gate with gore.

It retracted all of its limbs at once, carrying the decapitated man and his head into the grotto. There it peeled off the boots and clothing and chewed on the body. It saved the head for last, simply because it so enjoyed the man's expression of frozen astonishment.

Things above remained quiet for days, apart from the mournful tolling of church bells. All traffic on the bridge had ceased. Since there was no other way in and out of the walled town, it had only to wait.

On the fifth evening, the town gate creaked open a few feet and then slammed shut. Nervous bleating and four-legged patter on the cobblestones followed. It sent up one front limb to survey a lone, panicked sheep. The claw hovered over the animal for a long minute, regarding both the offering and the drawn faces of the observers who stood out of reach atop the walls. It snatched the sheep, shook the life out of the creature, and dropped the wooly corpse disdainfully on the cobbles. Below, it raised its beak above the water and, in a voice that made the bridge quiver, pronounced its first public speech:

"Not good enough."

The town went silent. Even the tolling of bells ceased.

At dusk on the sixth day, it heard the gate creak open again, and sent its claws up to investigate. A sleek heifer, bawling with reluctance, was goaded through the narrow opening by an old man wielding a long switch and wearing an expression of grim determination.

Before the old man had quite cleared the gate, its left claw snatched him and plunged him under water where it bit off the old fellow's right leg before returning him, spluttering and spouting blood, to the bridge. Meanwhile, it blocked the heifer's frantic gallop toward freedom with its right claw, swatting her into the river where she struggled against the swiftly moving current that swept her downstream.

It allowed a few moments for the observers on the town walls to take all this in, as well as for the old cowherd to finish bleeding to death.

"You can do better," it observed in a voice that made the stones shake.

Chewing at the leg — more gristle than meat yet carrying that delectable human taint — it waited and watched, its front claws perched on the bridge railings. The observers had withdrawn, leaving the old man's body for the crows, and nothing happened except for a flock of pigeons that erupted from the gate's guard tower and flew due south in the windless air as though following an unseen road in the sky.

Three days later, its afternoon doze was interrupted by a clatter of booted feet and the heavy footfall of horses stepping onto the bridge at the end opposite the town. The sun was low on the western horizon as it sent up its claws to observe twenty-odd foot soldiers armed with pikes, trundling along behind four helmeted men on caparisoned horses. The horses were giving their riders trouble, spooking at the huge, snake-like limbs hovering over them and staring at them with eyed claws.

The helmet of the man in front sported a bright bunch of plumes which wavered gaily back and forth as his horse shied. Wresting his steed under control, he rose in his stirrups to call out, in a voice that wavered only slightly, "Avaunt, foul water worms! Know you that I am Roderick of Illsley, sheriff and protector of this precinct, and have come at the behest of the citizens of Bournebury, to whose town you have laid siege."

It made a mental note to allow no more flights of pigeons. The sheriff continued: "I warn you now, depart at once, you and your serpent brethren, and return to whatever dark lair you came from, or face certain death!"

The eyes on the watching claws blinked. The waiting soldiers shifted uneasily.

There was a heavy quiet, and then a sound like a thousand cauldrons boiling simultaneously as the river turned to white froth. The bridge quavered and bounced; the riders struggled to prevent their mounts from bolting. The foot soldiers backed up several steps, careful not to slip in the muck churned up by the horses.

A chorus of terrified shrieks from atop the town walls refocused the small army's attention.

It anchored its tripod of tails on the river bottom and stretched to its full, looming height above the bridge. Its beaked head peered down balefully while its front limbs kept an eye on the gate guards at one end and the gawking soldiers at the other. Its other six limbs waved back and forth sinuously.

"You are mistaken," it drawled in a voice that caused the horses to flatten their ears. "There are no serpents here, and certainly no worms. There is only me. But that is quite enough."

The foot soldiers were running back down the road to Illsley before it finished speaking. It laughed, a huge huffing sound like boulders bouncing over a cliff. The men on horseback made a slightly more dignified retreat, ignoring the cries of dismay from the town walls as they cantered off.

It turned its gaze to the people on the walls, frozen into terrified silence. "Nice try," it said, "but only funny once. I'm getting hungry, by the way." With that, it withdrew into its grotto, leaving a pattern of whirlpools in its wake.

A dissonant blare of trumpets shattered the pre-dawn stillness. It raised its front claws expectantly. Torches burned from the gate towers, and a group of men stood huddled together on the parapet, grasping an upright, squirming bundle covered in sackcloth and bound with ropes. One of the men took a step forward, unfurled a trembling sheet of vellum, and bellowed a greeting.

"Oh fearsome sentry of the deep, the citizens of Bournebury respectfully crave a word with you," he began, reading from his scroll.

Intrigued, it sluiced itself out of its grotto and rose over the bridge. The man in front bowed several times as those behind him tightened their grip on the madly gyrating bundle. "Your presence here, while indeed an honor, presents a difficulty. We are cut off from supplies and have depleted our stores. We beseech you to consider our plight," he continued at the top of his lungs.

"You don't need to shout," it advised the man, in a voice that made the bundle cease its struggles and go limp. "My hearing is quite acute. Is that for me?" it enquired, waving one of its claws toward the cloth-bound figure.

"Um," replied the spokesman, thrown off his script.

"Let's see!" it urged, rubbing its front claws in anticipation. The men fumbled at the ropes and sackcloth. Their efforts revealed a blowsy woman of indeterminate age and disheveled hair. She roused as the fresh air hit her face, blinked her kohl-rimmed eyes, and passed out again.

The spokesman frantically scanned his page. "In surety of our pledge, we offer you this young maiden, the flower of our town . . ."

Its claw swept the woman off the wall and popped her into its eager mouth. The men on the parapet stood aghast as it chewed and gulped.

"Hmph," it remarked, its mouth full. "Hardly young, and the maiden status is doubtful. But you're getting closer. Let me know when you're ready to talk business." With that, it slipped back beneath the bridge.

There were two more days, and two more hapless sacrifices, each younger and comelier than her predecessor, before it consented to an agreement with the town. When it questioned the town fathers as to why all the victims were female, they assured it that this was in accordance with tradition. It found this quizzical, but of no consequence, and it understood the need to allow traffic over the bridge to flow unmolested. Otherwise Bournebury could fall prey to starvation and deprive it of its sustenance. Besides, subduing the town had obliged it to overeat, and it was uncomfortably full.

Twice a year thereafter, at the spring and fall equinoxes, it accepted a chosen victim under the age of twenty and, per the terms of the deal, free from disease or major blemish (it waived any maidenhood requirement as unnecessarily restrictive).

With little need to exert itself, the semiannual feedings were more than adequate. For three seasons of the year it guarded the bridge languidly, making sure the town's citizens didn't try any funny business. Some of the bolder and more foolhardy Bournebury youths made attempts to dispatch it during its winter dormancy, but as all of their efforts perforce involved breaking through river ice and thus awakening their target well before they could reach it with their swords or spears, the result was always the same: more wailing over empty caskets in the town, and extra meals for it, only accelerating its annual growth.

After three years of this, such doomed heroics were firmly suppressed by the town fathers, and it spent its winters below the bridge, dreaming of skinless princesses.

The town threw a nervous Welcome Back Festival for it each year, featuring music and pastries shaped like claws with eyes, culminating in the spring feeding. The sheriff was summoned from Illsley —a considerable bribe persuaded him to return — to observe how well the arrangement was working out, and traffic bustled across the bridge once again.

Thus life proceeded. Its town, as it had come to think of Bournebury, was sufficiently remote to be untroubled by much in the larger world. There was little to disturb the town, other than itself, besides the need to produce a surplus of daughters.

The molting process took longer as time passed, and wasn't always complete in time for the Festival, but it felt obligated to show up on cue and, in truth, it had come to look forward to the attention. Since the terms of the arrangement stipulated that no weapons be used against it, there was little cause for concern.

Then came a winter markedly warmer than usual, producing only a thin layer of river ice that broke up early. It twisted restlessly in its grotto, uncomfortably aware of its splitting, itching, peeling scales. When the equinox came and the sound of drums and pipes drifted down from atop the bridge, it was little more than halfway through its molt. It considered skipping the Festival altogether and just nabbing a milkmaid or even a fat farmer in another month or so. But the agreement had worked so well for so long, and any such violation was sure to cause a lot of bother, having to terrify the town into submission all over again and so forth. Really, the very thought was exhausting. Besides, no doubt its public was already gathered along the town walls, waiting for their annual spectacle.

Reminding itself that a good feeding always perked it up, it unfurled itself, stretched its limbs experimentally, blinked open all of its eyes, and launched itself out of the water with its usual panache. Drawing back its head, which now reached above the town gate, it let out a ground-bouncing roar, and uttered the customary words: "People of Bournebury, fulfill your oath. Deliver to me my tribute or face my retribution!"

It waited for the swell of music and the wailing that always accompanied the presentation of the sacrifice. Bound, blindfolded, and shrieking in terror, the damsel would be loaded into a large wicker basket hanging by a chain fastened to a stout beam projecting from the gate tower, specially built for this purpose. The town burghers, in full regalia, would cluster behind their bewigged mayor, who would read a brief statement — largely drowned out by the victim's screams — and then give the basket a good shove to send it swinging out to the end of the beam. This was its favorite part: it would bring its face close to sniff at the victim, as the drums pounded faster and faster. The shrilling pipes would rise in volume and tempo as the girl gibbered and pleaded. Just as the tension reached an unbearable pitch, it would utter some small witticism such as, "You smell delicious, my dear" and snatch her from the basket to swoop her down into the river, plucking off a leg or arm and devouring the tidbit appreciatively along the way.

But this time there was no wailing and no music. The chill wind whistled. The mayor and burghers stood huddled in their cloaks. The crowd watched from atop the town walls, stone-faced and silent. It felt unpleasantly cold where its soft interior was exposed.

Itself

It cleared its throat and roared. "People of Bournebury," it began, but was interrupted.

"Never mind all that, I'm right here," rang a small, clear voice from very nearby. It angled its head down to see the basket already in position at the end of the beam. Inside stood a wiry girl of about ten with untidy braids, wearing a grimy apron. Neither bound nor blindfolded, she chewed on a claw-shaped pastry.

"What's this?" it sputtered. It cast a glowering look at the mayor and burghers, who shrank back from their already safe distance. "This is hardly a proper sacrifice. She's skinny, and not very clean, and why isn't she tied up? Or screaming?"

"The lass is the only child of our recently deceased salt monger," called one of the burghers upon being elbowed by the mayor, "and is now, sadly, an orphan, who —"

"I said I'd do it," announced the girl.

It regarded her. "Well, that's a first," it remarked. "Feeding me is an honor the young ladies of Bournebury do not seem to appreciate."

"No, they don't," she acknowledged, finishing her pastry and reaching into the pocket of her apron.

"Then why volunteer?" it asked, its curiosity stronger than its appetite.

"You ate my cousin three years ago, and I didn't mind so much because she was stupid and stuck up, but last year you ate my auntie, and she was very nice and I loved her," she explained. "So now I'm going to kill you."

Its laugh reverberated in the stones. "And how do you propose to do that, my imp?" it asked. "I don't see any swords or pikes or even a wee bow and arrow anywhere on your scrawny person, and anyway, weapons aren't allowed. You are amusing for the moment, but that will soon pass. And then I'll EAT YOU, you do understand that, right? Feet first, in your case, due to your impertinence."

"No you won't, you'll be dead," she assured it, and from her apron pocket she flung a handful of something sparkly and white into its eyes.

"How dare . . . OW!" it howled. It had never felt real pain before. The experience was a shock.

"What are you . . . STOP THAT!" it bellowed, as the girl flung handful after handful of white granules at the eyes on its claws and the large patches on its body where its shell had yet to form properly. The pain was no longer a surprise: it was a searing explosion of agony. In confusion, it tried to fend off the rain of burning powder as its attacker grimly tossed the stuff at its most vulnerable regions: its still-naked limbs. It writhed and gasped, swinging ineffectually at the girl in the basket. An acrid smell filled its head. In its misery, it heard the girl speak.

"I *told* them this would work. I've been killing snails this way since I was three. You're just bigger. A big, nasty, mean snail-thing. All it takes is some salt."

It couldn't answer her, since its insides were bubbling and foaming into slimy rivulets across its bursting exterior. Its limbs had already shriveled to useless nubs. Its tails curled helplessly on the river bottom as the poison spread through its entrails. In a moaning, oozing ruin, it collapsed in upon itself and melted like a sodden pastry, leaving shell fragments and a foaming slick on the river's surface, swirling downstream.

The watching townspeople erupted in cheers. The wicker basket was hauled in and its occupant crowned with flowers and given another pastry. The whole town and all the folk in the surrounding countryside — in particular, the women — rejoiced.

And life in Bournebury proceeded with little to complain of beyond the effrontery of the salt merchant's daughter who, as her father's only survivor, maintained exclusive control of his inventory. Under her management the price of salt rose steeply, until she became quite the wealthiest resident of the town. Worse, she stubbornly refused to marry.

It was a continuing irritant to the city fathers, but there was little they could do. After all, nobody wanted to be without a ready supply of salt, just in case.

Naiad

by Victoria Nations

I had planned for a serendipitous discovery, one I could describe with mock surprise as I gloated on my fair fortune. The naysayers who dismissed me, who already questioned my value and judgment in the department, would be silenced.

I was quite certain of the preternatural world, the reality that lies past our sight. To deny its existence outright was a poor assessment of the evidence that had been collected. To declare it unnatural was a denial of our physical world. But a scientist does not simply believe without proof. Were I to make an outrageous claim without empirical evidence, I would be rightfully rebuked by my professional community. When I heard similar stories from laypeople, who asked me to believe on faith, I scoffed, as was appropriate.

Yet, I knew that creatures lived amongst us. I saw the hunched shadows hiding in dark corners. I heard the trees creak from strange beings squatting on their branches. Others were unwilling, or unable, to go to the lengths I would because they didn't have my insight. I would find irrefutable evidence because I was a monster, too.

I would silence the doubters and my critics. I would recover the prestige I once held. I would finally connect with them, the creatures that revealed themselves, but denied our kinship. They would welcome me as one of their own, drawn by my ability to walk in the human world, and through our union, my peers would have to acknowledge my truth. I would be denied no longer.

I kept these desires burning in my belly, a constant reminder of my task. I was meant for things less mundane than this.

I dressed in practical clothing, built for navigating the swamp and carrying the limited gear I required. After the path through the swamp ended, I went further. I followed the trails made by animals, skirting around knobbed cypress knees and hummocks, until only water extended under the trees.

I recorded the setting meticulously in my field notebook, knowing my notes would be mocked. The dean and his sycophants would laugh at my knowledge, until I presented the evidence I had gathered. That would stop their tongues. Would that it could stop their breath.

The swamp was still as I waded, and silent but for the sloshing around my calves. I stared into every break in the trees and into the dark water, where silt swirled with each step. The air was cool, but the water was as warm as a bath, as a body. Most of its residents were cold-blooded, so this was the warmth of rotting things, of putrescence and decay. Or, I hoped, something else.

When I spotted red darting through the murky water, I thought first of blood worms wriggling in the mud. But the red was there and gone. I stepped closer to find its source. I called as I walked, knowing she must be close to have shone so bright.

Bubbles, foamy and reeking, released from the mud as I walked. They gathered in greasy clumps on top of the water, sticking to larger nodules that bobbed up beside them. The shapes coalesced into fat nipples on her breasts, full and loose like the muck from which she rose. She emerged, face turned toward me.

My nymph. My chosen bride.

She was lush, a mass of mottled flesh and curves. She didn't beckon or swim teasingly away. She lay there limply, so still the water had no ripples. Bright eyes, streaked with yellow, stared at me through snarls of hair.

Looking at her tried my soul.

I felt the madness others had reported from their alleged experiences. I pulled out my field notebook, desperate for notation, to capture all I was seeing and feeling. I fought to be impartial rather than blithering imprecise details or overly dramatic descriptions.

But my eyes pulled back to watch her float there, sodden and bloated. I imagined breathing life into her, this seemingly drowned girl. She tracked my movements as if she knew I wanted to reach for her. Dazzling yellow eyes locked with mine as her curved mouth opened.

Her split red tongue flickered from her parted lips. She tapped it against them. Tantalizing. Luring. I gasped, and her mouth opened wider in response. Wanton. Threatening.

Her beak was sharp against my wrist when she bit. A gift I hadn't realized I craved. Wounds are irrefutable.

The muck loosened the more we moved. My hair was soon plaited with strings of it. I could not tell if my chest was tight from her squeezing embrace or the mud closing in. I planned to note how the mud cooled the deeper I sank, how I still burned despite the cold.

I plan to pull myself out one day, boots full of leaves and water, clothes sticking to me, warm rot burning inside me despite the cool air. I will scrub the dirt from my skin and hair, and I will show the doubters my victory, my proof, and they will regret their dismissal of me.

But the nip of her hard mouth holds me back. Bits of me have been lost to the swamp, to her. My discovery exceeded my hopes. To say I was anointed with knowledge both dreadful and sublime would be true.

I would argue with my putative fellows, were I wont to, were I *able* to, that they will never earn the glory of truth with their meager efforts, as I have.

My truth: I am unsalvageable, smoldering here beside her, cooking in the mud.

Cirrata

by K. F. Hartless

When the leaves turn upside down and shake their pale bellies in the wind, I'm done for. Normally, if there's a chance of rain, the slightest drizzle, I stay within a five-mile radius of home. Once I'm in my apartment, I toss the cursed thing in the closet, ignore the knocking, and wait for the storm to stop.

Master is smart. It knows today I ventured outside the safety zone to present my latest model to clients. Wealthy entrepreneurs don't understand why an up-and-coming architect would want to unveil her most precious design remotely.

As I pass the Mercury Fountain, I admire the nozzles winding around the structure, leading my eye straight to the messenger perched at the pinnacle. He balances on one foot as if about to take off on his next mission.

Without warning, the wind flips me the bird. The vessel flutters against my leg. Master twitches, yearning to be lifted, flexed, set free. Under my breath, I curse Aunt

Edith, the impending storm, but most of all, my lack of free will.

When my mother asked me to help her keep vigil, I tried to get out of it. I rationalized that hospice had been called in and they were best equipped to handle this sort of thing. Aunt Edith's breath grew shallower each day, and she'd stopped taking liquids. But my mother was persistent.

"I expect you'll act the same when my time comes. You know, Eddy was a second mom to you." True enough. Aunt Edith had no children of her own, so I was the closest thing she'd had to a daughter. In the end, I couldn't refuse.

Mother and I took shifts. I kept Aunt Eddy company in the mornings, scrolling through *Architectural Digest Magazine* and sketching rudimentary designs. A briny smell permeated her bedroom despite the open window. Was it the sour smell of death or the ointment hospice workers rubbed on her papery skin while watching their daytime soaps? I wasn't sure. But for two days, Aunt Edith remained still. A steady morphine drip kept her comfortable. That is until the third day, when thunder rumbled the floorboards. I paused my sketch to find Aunt Eddy sitting up in her bed, licking her fingers and smoothing a few stray hairs as if she'd returned from a windy excursion on one of her many cruises.

I peed myself a little at the sight of her, upright, smiling serenely as she asked, "Nora, sweetheart, what's being served for our supper?"

I texted my mom. *She's awake. Come now! A miracle.*

"Oh, Aunt Eddy! Would you like broth?" I said, wondering if it was wise to offer, but broth seemed like the sort of thing you fed someone who up until a minute ago had been on death's doorstep. When she didn't answer and kept grooming herself, I searched my bag for the number to the hospice. Oh, what time did that nurse say she'd be back from her break?

"Come closer, Nora. dear. The weather is calm." Thunder outside said otherwise, but I made my way to Aunt Eddy's bed.

She tilted her cheek as she'd always done since I was little, and I dutifully kissed the sagging skin, wet with fever. Then, she leaned toward me as if to speak a secret in my ear, but the voice I heard next was not of this world.

"Cirrata! Cirrata!" Aunt Edith spat as she spoke. "Bad cuss to you!"

I stepped back, frightened by her sudden change in pitch and volume. She pointed her wet, knobby finger, straight at my chest.

"The first drops quench." Aunt Eddy reached under her bed.

"Are you warm, Aunt Eddy?" I was texting like crazy now. SOS. The scream emoji, anything to get my mother's attention.

"Boils your bowels." She returned with a green, eel-like smile, something black and bunched on her lap.

"Siphons your soul." A stroke of lightning. The morphine. The drip must have run out. That was the only explanation. The nurse said I could up the dose if there was any sign of distress. Well, this certainly qualified. I made my way to the other side of the bed to see if I could figure out the mechanism. This was a fit of madness, a delusion, nothing more.

Before I could press the button on the feed, Aunt Edith lifted the object in the air. An ordinary umbrella. Black, save for a dark, wooden handle. She fumbled with the button securing the fabric and when she finally freed it, she tried opening the canopy overtop herself. But her muscles were too fatigued. Her brows joined together when she couldn't force it up.

"Aunt Eddy, please, let me help you." But, as soon as I took hold of the base and forced the shaft, she collapsed back on her bed. Still and white and pale.

I shook her, but no movement. No breath. In shock, I stood over her corpse with the umbrella until my mother arrived, as if it were my job to keep her body dry from some unseen storm.

From that moment on, the unholy umbrella was my burden.

My mother and I were the last to leave the graveyard at Aunt Eddy's funeral.

"Everything went great, Mom."

"I'd planned to say something about her gardening club. I'd rehearsed every word, but..." Rumbles in the sky sent a chill down my back as I remembered Aunt Edith's last words.

Fat drops fell.

"Sort of storm gets worse before it gets better," I patted her shoulder, but Mom didn't budge.

"I can't leave her like this. Here, give me your umbrella, you go on back to the car."

She grabbed at the handle, but I kept my grip on it. Soon, we were playing tug-of-war on Eddy's grave.

"It's not how long you grieve that counts," I said, tugging the handle loose.

"Well, the least you can do is hold the damn thing over my head while I say my goodbye." I opened the umbrella while she knelt to place a white rose by Eddy's headstone.

"You can come back anytime," I said, as a tentacle, cold and curving, slithered from the black shell above my mother. Slimy suckers encircled her throat, pointing outward like an oversized pearl necklace.

Before I could pull the tentacle off, a second one plunged into her mouth. Then a third and fourth entered her eyes. The creature, which appeared to be an octopus, was tasting my mother, eating my mother, who moaned as I tugged on the tentacles. The slippery appendages suffocated her, and I was powerless to stop them. Master's limbs burrowed into my mother's orifices.

I dropped the umbrella to try and run for help, but mother's hand jutted out to catch the rod. I tried to pry her fingers loose, but the object seemed fused. I continued to tug on Master's appendages, but it only made the monster dig in deeper. Desperate, I took the keys from my pocket and tried to slice the limb in her mouth free, but I couldn't seem to scrape a single, slippery sucker loose.

Without warning, Mother took off through the graveyard with the umbrella overhead. A twisted Mary Poppins, she leapt the tops of the gravestones, hopped urns. From across the cemetery, I looked on in horror as she positioned her neck above a spike on the cemetery's wrought-iron fence.

"Wait! At least tell me your name. I beg you!" The creature paused, while I extended my upturned hands. "Please. Anything but her."

I didn't hear a reply out loud, but felt it, like a punch to the gut.

"Cirrata? Is that you?" But it was too late. The sharp edge of the spike punctured her neck, and blood spritzed over the century-old wrought-iron. I was on my knees, winded from the chase, as the only person in the world who loved me unconditionally bled out on a cemetery fencepost.

Cirrata used its appendages to roll my mother's head clean off. It wrapped around every surface of her face, sucking her dry. Hair, sinew, cartilage, and brain tissue leaked from her face. What fell to the ground when the

Master was through with her was bare bone, a husk of a human, and nothing else.

Headless, Mother stood clutching the dark umbrella. Once shock receded, I went to her, wrapped my arms around her waist, and sobbed my apologies as a bloody tentacle alighted on my forehead to stroke my bangs clear from my eyes. When I took hold of the handle, my mother's body sank to the ground.

After Mother's funeral, I tried to throw the vile thing away. Tossed it on the compost, atop the wilted flowers and burnt-out pillars from her wake. There'd been a forecast of rain that never materialized. When the trashman came, I heard shrieks of agony. I witnessed his decapitation from the living room window. The next time I went to my car, the cirrata was already inside, camouflaged against the dashboard.

Desperate, I tied a weight to the rod and cast it out to sea, but the next morning, the damned device sat on my doorstep, a tangle of seaweed attached to its tip.

After that, I got reckless. I set the damn thing on fire, watching the flames consume the fabric down to the metal frame. My heart sank when I spotted it on the counter a couple of hours later, wet flaps sprawled on the granite like a giant Rorschach blot.

My last attempt was to stuff the cursed thing into the trash compactor, grinding the fabric to bits. But that same evening, as I cleared a circular spot on the mirror to check for stray chin hairs, I saw it for the first time. Perched on the rack, it peered over the edges of a terracotta towel.

Master remembers faces. If you catch its eye, you better hope it likes you.

In the passing months, I abandoned any hopes of ridding myself of the cursed umbrella and instead researched cirrata. The creature preferred to be called Master. And demanded I take it with me anytime I left the apartment. I came to believe that the umbrella was the creature's shell, essential to its survival, and nothing I did was going to separate the two.

Three hearts: my research taught me that Master has three blood pumping organs. I tell myself that's why it's greedy. Why it feeds so often, to keep those three hearts beating in rhythm.

Mother's death muted my senses. By killing her, Master shot me with its ink and dulled all the colors and flavors around me. Without a doubt, my aunt had cursed me on her deathbed. And if I didn't want to be consumed, I must be its caretaker, regardless of the costs.

I changed my routines, worked from home as much as possible, and since the abominable thing followed me everywhere, I tried to ensure I had no use for it. Keeping out precipitation became of paramount importance. Once opened, the umbrella could not be closed without some bloody tithe.

Cirrata's red eyes peer through the nylon panels, monitoring and learning. Master is smart. I am kept alive to host its hunger, and if I do not amuse it at regular intervals, it will leave me as lifeless as my mother.

Sure, there's been a couple of close calls. My neighbor's son wandered into the coat closet. I caught him fidgeting with the handle, lifting and releasing the stem.

I snatched it from him as fast as I could, wagging it as I spoke. "Never open umbrellas indoors. Do you hear me?"

And when his mother gaped at me, I added, "It's terrible luck, you know."

After that, I put a lock on the hall closet. Disgruntled, the knocks intensified. Only removing the mechanism pacified Master.

Today in the park, a tongue-like tentacle toys with my ear. Master is thirsty. Here in the dank square, no creatures stir that can comfort it. Well, only me and Magee, the homeless woman who sleeps on the park's one rotting bench.

Drenched already, she lies still by the fountain. I see her each time I cut through the park on my commute. The smell of piss and filth keeps most of the walkers at bay, but I've always tried to leave her snacks and toiletry items. A little kindness costs me nothing.

Magee won't leave her bench, determined to keep her spot from any other stragglers who might pass through.

A tentacle enters my right earlobe. The rain increases. There isn't time to wait. I go to Magee, fan the umbrella over her, knowing the devil lurks inside, knowing full-well what it intends to do.

I clear my throat. "Staying dry, Magee?" The damp is thick. I hope she won't answer.

"It's not stolen." She replies, clutching her raincoat.

"No, the storm. Here, take it." I offer her the handle.

"Thanks. Don't need it." She rolls into the corner of the bench. Master enters my right ear, deeper than ever before. His suction cups tickle. An inch further and the drum will explode.

"Don't be silly," I say, nudging her with the curved base of the handle. "It's only going to get worse."

The handle burns my skin. I'm running out of time, but I don't dare let go.

Magee rolls over. Maybe she wants the free shower. Her downturned expression says she is less than amused.

"Fine. If it means you'll leave."

She moves to a sitting position on the bench, and the light from the lamppost finds her features. Her eyes. Here in the heavy torrents of rain, they look redder than Master's. My heartbeat thuds into the rod as I extend it her way, simultaneously hoping that she takes it and that she runs from me screaming.

Shapes blur in the rain's haze. Closer to Magee, I can see pain in her movements, the kind of suffering that excites the Master who twitches below the umbrella's tip.

"You can go now." She tilts the umbrella in my direction, nudges it toward me as if to shoo me away.

"Bad cuss to you!" The words surprise me, even as they exit my throat.

I rationalize that this is supposed to happen, and yet it's my punishment to watch as the Master's tentacles encircle Magee's neck.

"What the...What have you given me?" Magee's screams excite Master, who is quick to begin mining her ears.

"The first drops quench." I drop my shawl, let the raindrops find hiding spots in the fields of my hair.

"Boils your bowels." I'm not as strong as Aunt Eddy. I must rid myself of this creature before the guilt of what I've done eats me alive.

I deserve dampness. The creeping cold on my spine. I deserve much worse. And watching Magee suffocate, I panic. Try to undo what I've done by not saying the final words.

I yank the umbrella, watch as it turns inside out. And for the first time I see Master, exposed atop his shell. It's the first time I've seen the cirrata's full form. In the center of its bulbous head, glowing cinders. It is larger than I could have imagined, and its tentacles rest in the bowl of the upside-down umbrella.

I fumble with a lighter from my coat pocket. I manage to get a flame. I press the fire to the upside-down umbrella. Flames consume the fabric, but not fast enough. Master slinks onto the wet pavement. An adept shapeshifter, it transforms into a frog and pulses away.

"Siphons your soul," I say. Thinking that's it, until I realize Magee's fingers are fused to the handle, as my mother's were. Magee can't let go, and the fire inches closer.

I try to pry her fingers loose, but I have no way of hacking the wretched umbrella off. I watch horrified as the fire spreads from handle to hand. Magee makes a deep, guttural noise. The rain can't conquer the flames, which consume first her forearm, then her bicep. What's worse, in my panic, I've lost track of Master.

The fountain. Stupid. I hadn't been thinking and, in a moment, I pull Magee's mangled coat toward the wide basin.

"I can't swim."

This is absurd, as the fountain is a few feet deep, but I do my best to reassure her.

"I won't let you drown, Magee." True enough. She's my ticket out of this mess.

I hold her under for less than a minute, until the flames become bubbles. When she emerges, her inky, black pupils look like dirty water droplets.

Blackness leaks from her mouth. Tentacles twist her legs and torso, top to bottom like a tourniquet.

Magee reaches into the murky water and grabs Master's head. She manages to lift the bulbous cranium above the surface. When cirrata are agitated, their skin turns bright red, and Master's is boiling cinnabar.

"Hold tight," I say, reaching over the edge of the fountain to take a huge bite. Chunks of Master's flesh come off in my teeth. I chew and chew until I'm able to swallow, not sure if spitting him out will stop him. Holding back a gag, I take another mouthful.

Magee never loosens her grip. Several bites in, Master's tentacles go limp. I let go of my grip on Magee's coat.

"Is it dead?" I don't expect a response.

Magee replies with a smile. Her teeth are curved, black scimitars, stained from Master's dye.

"Let me pull you out." I reach over the edge of the fountain. Magee pushes away.

"No thanks."

Would she join Master on the bottom? I ignore her and pull harder at her coat, but she's heavier than me, and I can't get her body out of the basin.

Within minutes, I'm alone in the park. Drenched, but no longer a prisoner.

A baptism of sorts. What's done can't be undone, and perhaps in time, I will atone for all of it.

Everything You Dump Here Ends Up in the Ocean

by Anemone Moss

The moon is already high and full, reflecting in bright ribbons off the waves around us, by the time she takes me on board her platform. It's an old oil platform, long since stripped of industrial equipment and roughneck accouterments in favor of the sleek, streamlined whites and reds of custom-manufactured scientific R&D machinery, specially designed to tickle the fancy of Silicon Valley investors desperate to stave off social unrest with images of a green, capitalist future. I knew she was a grifter even before I saw it, but not the sort simply looking to fill a garage with expensive cars; she has her own intentions aside and apart from those of the investing class, and tonight she's promised me a glimpse of them.

"I've always found myself drawn to trash," she says in her nebulously aristocratic way. "First as an artist, and then as a researcher. Even in my private life, it fascinates me, what we've collectively abandoned as a society, which then must bear witness to us."

On the trip over from the marina she explained how she had selected this site, how the local eddies of the coastline consolidated to make a small garbage patch here, a microcosmic galaxy of drifting refuse that would be the prototype for a plastic-mitigation project she planned to enact in the larger garbage patches of the seas. One day, she said, the whole world would see the outcome of what was beginning here. A great speech which every would-be innovator made, but her certainty and the audacity in her eyes made it hard to challenge her, despite her suspicious refusal to share the contents of her research.

Now she's leading me along the edge of the platform, only an iron railing holding me back from a perilous drop into the night water. With the flick of a remote, floodlights illuminate the bluegreen waves far below. Her hand drifts over mine, the softest of touches. "Do you see what I've done already?"

"It's amazing." She showed me the pictures, how plastic waste once spiraled and churned in the tide nearby, and if the photographs are not doctored, and if her claims that she didn't mechanically remove any of it are true, then she really has developed a biological method to produce the clean water around us, marked only by the seaweed which clusters in lazy, bulbous shadows.

I'm genuinely impressed, more than I expected to be. My reasons for coming here had become muddled. When I first met her, I felt the activist stirring inside me, my instinctive suspicion of wealth and capital, my dire environmental concerns about the sea I'd so loved as a child. But through our frequent meetings, I had come to think of her as a skillful scam artist, and a deeply charming one at that. Perhaps she knew my initial suspicions and simply didn't care; she seemed to want to show me her lab more as a matter of pride than as a resolution to any of the ideological debates we shared over dinner.

She turns the lights off, and for a moment my eyes are plunged into night-blindness. Slowly the outlines of the platform and her body, illuminated by red lighting and the distant glow of the moon, return to me. Distantly, something large splashes in the water beneath us, and my thoughts turn to the sea lions which gather around the marina barking like dogs. Do they swim out here at night?

"Marine biology was my first passion," she says. "I'm grateful for the opportunity to return to it."

"How did that happen?" I ask. "You were an artist, right? In New York?"

"Oh, I can't reveal all my secrets yet," she says, and though I can't see her face, I know she's making that sly smile. "Come below, to the wet lab."

She insists I put on a wetsuit before we go down. Somehow, she has one prepared in just my size. I should be frightened when she does things like this, but I'm charmed—to be attended to, to be another of her projects. She knew in advance she would invite me over tonight, and had somehow clandestinely taken or guessed my measurements and spent the whole evening carefully positioning the pieces so that I would be the one to insist she show me her work. I'm honored to be in the grasp of such a meticulous manipulator, a woman after my own heart. Someone who knows what she wants, and knows how to get it. Or, perhaps, has just recognized the passion burning in me.

I change in a small dressing room, leaving my evening wear in a smooth, clean locker that only vaguely smells of algae and chlorinated disinfectant. The sea smell is intoxicating to me, harkening back to a simpler time in my life, my first love, as a child, of the depths and the unknown creatures deep within them. As I worm my legs into the rubbery second skin, I smile at the tentacles tattooed across my tits, delicately disguising the stretch marks and scars from my difficult recovery after breast enhancement surgery. If she's lucky, she'll get to see those tattoos tonight.

"Now, I know I already asked you to leave your devices on the boat," she says from beyond the privacy curtain, "but I have to insist that if you have anything metallic at all you leave it in the locker. It's not only a matter of my personal data security, it's the sensitivity of some of the... equipment below."

There goes my necklace, a little pentagram, remnant of my short wiccan phase from years before. I wore it religiously when I first transitioned, and ever since it's been a lucky talisman.

She's also suited up when I join her in the dimly lit room. Once she finishes eyeing me up and down, she opens the hatch in the center of the floor without a word. I can feel her silent approval. I work hard to maintain my figure, and I fought through years of bigotry to achieve it, a subject the two of us have discussed at length. Indeed, it was her undisguised admiration of my transformative process that first got me more interested in her bed than her lab.

She gestures to the ladder below our feet: "Let's descend."

We're now in a peaceful indoor pool, the floor beneath us gently sloping further into the water, lit only by red lights along the walls and small, ultraviolet LEDs hanging over trellises of tangled blackgreen mesh which look something like seaweed, something like fishing nets. The room could be a nightmare version of a grow room, except for the water coming up to our waists. Little, gray amphipods dart around the plantlike netting to either side of us, responding to any movement or sound we make. The water is cold, but warmer than I expected.

"The world is doomed, but you already know that," she says.

"Is this your stump speech?" I ask.

"No, not at all. I saved this just for you. This is the truth."

Something drifts past me in the water. At first I think it's a plastic bag, but then I make out the trailing tentacles, iridescent in the red and ultraviolet lighting. The tentacles momentarily latch onto my wetsuit when they brush past my leg, and I know that little stinging cells are uselessly sending microscopic darts filled with poison into the rubber of my suit. The dark, triangular design on the top of the jellyfish's bell looks like the Albertson's grocery store logo.

"I know you know this because I looked into your past." She closes the space between us, and I feel my heartbeat rise. "You used to be quite the eco-extremist. Against civilization, against Leviathan, wasn't it?"

"Something like that," I say, trying not to lose my cool. As my eyes adjust to the ultraviolet vibrations, I realize there are more jellyfish drifting around, different sizes and colors, all with that same iridescent texture like an oil slick. There's a mild anesthetic tingle on my exposed feet, almost painful. "So, are you worried I'm some kind of terrorist, here to destroy all your hard work?"

Her fingers, firm but not harsh, coil around my wrist. "I'm not worried about you at all. I need someone with a radical vision for change. You know, I really like you."

As always, I don't know what to read in her face, her perfectly composed expression. She's smiling, and the terror in my gut makes me want to kiss her more. Better to prolong it; rich girls aren't easily swayed by emotional bonds. "You need me, huh?"

"Do you know my secret? I'm a horrible researcher."

At the far end of the room, where the water grows deeper, there's less light. She's gently leading me there. My body is buzzing with anxiety, sensitive to any movement through the water.

"After I was discovered, I tried to bring together a team of scientists to understand what was happening. They lacked the conviction needed."

Now I can see the back wall. Four human bodies in various stages of decay and skeletonization are fused to the wall by some kind of resin, overtaken by invertebrate lifeforms: mussels and barnacles covering their bones, crabs crawling in and out of flesh. The intricate, feathery arms of fractal starfish cluster on the lower halves of their bodies, submerged beneath the water.

My heart sinks, and reflexively the words, so cliché, spill out of me: "Please, I don't want to die."

There's nothing more to plead. I have no family, no life outside of this, no real friends anymore. I lost it all in the process of the life I tried to live. Images flash before me, childhood friends mocking and betraying me, my wife leaving me when I started to transition, being fired from my job, fleeing my home, dropping out of college, comrades kettled and incarcerated, friends overdosing, losing job after job just trying to stay afloat. A lifetime of becoming human garbage, and now I'm flushed out to sea with the rest of the trash.

"Good," she says. "I don't want you to die. It was an unpleasant experience I wouldn't wish on anyone else."

I want to flee but where would I go? She has the key to the boat's cabin. I could try to break into it, but I suspect the glass is bulletproof, and that's only if I could get past her. Maybe I could find an EPIRB somewhere, activate it, and summon the coast guard...

"Come, I want to show you everything you've ever dreamed of," she says and gestures to a hatch at the far end of the room, guarded on either side by dead researchers. Her voice is so alluring, and the terror in my heart is so great, that it almost stops my dawning awareness of the vast and dismal horror of my dreams in recent years.

Passing between those four grim corpses, four horsemen of an apocalypse unknown to Christianity, my experience turns psychedelic, my flesh overstimulated, almost feverish. Fear traces glistening lines of light over our movements, turning her soft words into susurrations from a gentle shoreline kissed with waves.

"My scientists determined it started as a virus. The evolutionary advantage of a virus is its capacity to mutate. The disadvantage is its lack of options; its domain is only the synthesis of a few proteins and what they can do."

We are walking through what was once a proper and well-equipped laboratory, but the microscopes are overgrown with slime, the specimen jars are teeming with life, the incubators hang open as strange, gaunt fish dart in and out, and clear tendrils worm across the walls and ceilings, a chandelier of jelly hanging from each bright UV light.

"But out at sea, exposed to so many mutagens and so many new organic polymers, the modern, chemical miracle of plastics, something came to be, a virus whose strategy is symbiotic, relying on its extreme and unparalleled affinity for horizontal gene transfer. A new form of life."

The submerged work desks are covered in encrustations of coral, totally impossible in the limited time this lab has been operational. They look almost like clusters of styrofoam riddled with holes, filled with life. One of them slowly floats away, its jagged back undulating.

"I don't know precisely when I came to be, but I know how I came to be as I am now. A woman was killed by a man she'd arranged a date with on Grindr and a friend of his. They wrapped her corpse in garbage bags and dumped her in these salty waters... with no idea of what they'd initiated. And with that body, I was born in the depths. As the last signals in that brain were fading to oblivion, something connected with those neurons, something between the water and the plastic bag. I am what remains."

As she leads me further into the lab, we continue into deeper and deeper water, pressure around my stomach now and strange, lovely buoyancy almost tickling me from below. Through the rippling water I can see clams growing from the floor with strangely regular geometry, and something like a transparent octopus darting quickly along. Instead of a head, it seems to have a network of interconnected tentacles, making it look like the discarded plastic rings of a six-pack.

"It found me, and from me it found what it had lacked: purpose. Together we dreamed of growing. Do you know that many invertebrates have a decentralized nervous system? In some ways, I think this brain of mine is a weakness."

My next step finds no floor beneath me, only water, and I frantically kick to stay afloat.

"Don't worry," she says. "I don't think you're at risk of drowning now, or ever again."

There's that same sly smile of hers, and that's when it all hits me with a sudden wave of realization, like waking from a bad dream. The dream of being a lonely, isolated organism. The jellyfish, drifting past me earlier, injecting my feet... and my rubber wetsuit. The strange tingling in my body, yes it was fear, but it was also something else. I can feel it as the nerves in my skin connect with the nerves growing in the wetsuit. I can feel as flesh the silicon in my implants, feel the body of my wetsuit, truly a second skin now, as the water moves around it. But more than that: I can feel the creatures in the water, from the large eels hiding behind the desks to the microscopic plankton drifting around us, the jellyfish in the other room, the corpses on the wall, unable to hold onto their own selves, but in death host to a new form of life. And I feel *her*, her warmth, her presence, her body, her mind. And beneath us, something deep and vast. Connected now to me, to the microplastics in every cell of my body.

Are you ready now? I feel her voice blossoming in our shared mind.

Yes. I am ready.

We go below the platform, down into the water, slowly sinking. When the seawater first enters my lungs it's a shock, but not too great of one, since she has experienced it many times before. Soon I am comfortable letting the last bubbles of air out. Drifting down, I am warm in the suit, feeling almost like a seal in its layer of blubber as my body assimilates it, as it assimilates my body. Beneath the platform extends a vast web of plastic flesh: nets and straws and bags and bottles all filtering for plankton and growing algae and transmitting soft, friendly signals to my nervous system through the network of microbes in the water. We spiral down through the intricate labyrinth of webbing that has grown beneath the platform, into the deeper dark. My eyes adjust better than they ever could have before, still making out faint traces of light in even the deep blackness of the night water. I can feel the spirits of the deep drifting past me, not only the squid and the fishes but also clothes lost from a lonely child, tires abandoned and rolled off a cliff, chunks of a broken surfboard, fast food containers, everything whirling around me like a carnival parade of ghosts, dead memories of the human world, sprouting compound eyes and segmented legs, growing muscles to swim, gills to breathe, mouths to eat. Abandoned bits of human lives fragmented and repurposed as the flesh of the sea.

And then I feel it, turning its awareness to me. Impossible to describe what it is: an underwater volcano; a dozen whalefalls; a sea slug the size of a city; a lost nuclear submarine; a benevolent tumor of nervous tissue capable of calculations greater than any computer. It is all these things and more. It smells like my lover, or perhaps she always smelled of it. It sends out complex electromagnetic patterns expertly shielded from the seeking sensors of the world's navies and scientists. It is both the conductor of the orchestra and the product of a billion minds. A tremendous, heaping, teeming mass of living trash at the bottom of the ocean.

I know then why she selected me, why this was always my fate. My research into global logistics networks, my vision for the end of the world, my hatred of the society that had tortured and abandoned me: it is taking all of this into itself, spreading the buried and repressed components of my consciousness through gulper eels with polyethylene bones and sharks with vinyl skin. The plan is so much further underway than I ever could have guessed, sprawling from this core to other growing polyps across the seafloor, preparing for the next stage in its maturity. Preparing for the open water.

We have already almost reached the fiber-optic cables connected to the internet and the power grids, she thinks to me. *Soon all the land will be choked by the trash it has sent out here and given a new life. And then, we will no longer be doomed.*

At that I smile. This night has gone well after all, far better than I expected. I feel the ocean all around me, filled with myriad, new creatures.

At last, I think, *the world is waking up.*

There is Something Sleeping in the Mariana Trench; It Dreams of You

By Bridget D. Brave

There's something sleeping in the Mariana Trench right now, some 36,000 feet below the waves.

You do know about the Mariana Trench, don't you? I feel that anyone with an internet connection and a modicum of curiosity has seen a video, or perhaps an artfully-designed image describing its impossible depths.

The Mariana Trench is approximately seven miles deep. It was once believed to be the deepest part of the ocean, but now we know better. It's still plenty deep, however. You could stack 100,000 Statues of Liberty, one on top of another, and still need another sixteen thousand Statues for your unruly and, frankly, *wasteful* tower to be visible from the ocean's surface.

The Mariana Trench is *deep*. It is deep and dark and almost impossible to fathom. And there, in that unfathomable darkness, something stirs in its sleep. It turns uneasily onto its side. Its multiple eyelids flutter in the pitch-black. Perhaps it makes a satisfied, sleepy, smacking sound with its ruined lips.

It dreams of you.

"But, why?" You might ask. "Why would a creature so impossibly deep, a creature who could not bear to look at the sunlight, let alone understand what sunlight *is*, dream of someone like me? Someone who lives and goes about their days not in the water, but on dry land?"

That question is unimportant.

Did you know whales are thought to dive to the depths of the Mariana Trench? Scientists have recorded strange, haunting sounds from that deep, dark crevasse. They explained those sounds as "whales, probably."

Those scientists are wrong. Whales would never venture to this part of the Trench. Whales know better.

Perhaps the scientists already know this. Perhaps they've glimpsed some fragment of the truth, some flash of movement visible on the green-tinted screens they stare into, unable to view the ocean floor at such depth with their naked eyes. Perhaps they turn from that vision, not wanting to see, shutting their eyes tight as a stray tentacle brushes across their robotic camera's lenses. Not wanting to know what that tentacle is attached to, or why the claws at the end appear to jut from appendages that one could almost describe as "fingerlike." Perhaps they cling to the safety of "whales, probably" to keep themselves from reckoning with What They Saw.

There is no creature with fingers at the ends of its tentacles. There is nothing at the bottom of the Mariana Trench that can mimic exactly the sound their mothers made when they cried late at night, when those mothers thought no one could hear. There is no creature who knows their deepest fears, or the exact moment of their deaths, and where did they get that idea, anyway?

Those scientists probably just need more sleep.

The thing that sleeps at the bottom of the Mariana Trench does not need more sleep. It's always very, *very* well-rested. It sleeps now because it enjoys dreaming. And, as we know, tonight those dreams are of you.

"But," you might sputter, "that doesn't make any sense! Why me?"

I told you, that question doesn't matter. Stop asking it. There is no answer that will satisfy you.

Did you know that orca can dive up to 850 feet before they need to resurface? The Mariana Trench is twelve times deeper than that. Did you know that orcas have an extra section of their brain which we don't entirely understand? It's called the "paralimbic region." Researchers believe it has something to do with processing emotion, perhaps additional computing power for cognitive function. But they can't be entirely sure.

Research can be a real mixed bag, you know.

The thing that sleeps at the bottom of the Mariana Trench has five such regions. Regions we would recognize as lobular and familiar structures of the brain, but ones we could not imagine the use for.

There is Something Sleeping in the Mariana Trench; It Dreams of You

The thing at the bottom of the Mariana Trench knows *exactly* what those regions are used for, and how to use them. It has seen what it can do with those regions, the pain it can inflict, even from a great distance. It knows the suggestions a person would need to, say, book an unexpected ocean voyage. Or perhaps a beach vacation to a remote island with a sharp drop-off just outside the swimming region. It knows when to make those suggestions, and how to make it seem as if it were your idea, all along.

It knows many things that would astonish you.

It watched as you spread butter across toast on a hand-me-down plate on the stained counter of your first apartment, all those months and months ago. It knows the fear that strikes when an unexplained pain registers in your rib cage. Is that your heart? Your lung? Another organ? You are never entirely sure of the exact location of any of your organs, did you know that? It's difficult to tell from anatomy sketches, and our bodies tend to have an almost jellyfish-like tendency to move and flow, insides shifting and moving as we grow into our unique shapes. Without carefully peeling back the skin and parting the musculature, without cracking open your chest cavity and delving inside, it's truly impossible to know.

Do you know where your spleen is right now? The answer might surprise you.

The answer wouldn't surprise the thing that sleeps at the bottom of the Mariana Trench. That thing knows the precise location of each of your organs. It knows what your insides would look like, were your skin and muscles ripped roughly away from your torso's connective tissue. It knows which of your ribs to break off to find each pink and purple, slippery glob of internal flesh. It knows which ones are delicious, and which ones are nutritious enough not to worry about the unpleasant taste. Its mouth even now fills with saliva - an impressive feat for a creature surrounded by so much water. It can taste the tang of blood-soaked membrane parting with surgical precision beneath its rows of razor-sharp teeth.

It hungers for you.

Did you know that the average pressure per inch in the Mariana Trench is almost 15 pounds? That's enough to crush the hull of a cruise ship. It's enough to crumple a tank. A creature would have to be very, very tough to survive those depths. Tough as titanium.

The thing that sleeps at the bottom of the Mariana Trench is twice as tough as that.

Most sea life at that depth cannot withstand the pressure at the surface as a result of their unique anatomy. Bringing a creature from the Trench to the surface would result in it becoming a pile of jelly, melting unpleasantly into the deck of your boat, only a memory of its original form.

The thing that sleeps at the bottom of the Mariana Trench has no such limitations. Its original form - massive and slithering in the dark - would look much the same on the deck of your ship, had you a ship large enough to hold it.

You might sigh in relief now. You're not some ridiculous billionaire with a megayacht, nor do you live on one of those floating island luxury cruise ships. That thing at the bottom of the trench can dream about you, but it's not like you have a chance of actually encountering it.

Maybe not today. Maybe not even this year, or the next. But there is a part of the thing's mind that knows you are wrong.

There is a part of the thing's mind that already sees your future. That knows its time will come, that there will be a day when you have forgotten that you read this warning, that there will be a day when you venture into a part of the ocean where it can slip up from its craggy hideaway and silently weave through the waves, to find where your toe carelessly hangs above the shining surface of the water. It already sees itself uncoiling one of its hundreds of tentacles and reaching for that toe, its seven-jointed fingers curling in anticipation, lamprey-like mouth yawning open, incomprehensibly wide, and ringed with thousands of ragged-edged teeth.

It knows that day is not today.

But it's not worried, nor is it restless.

The thing that sleeps at the bottom of the Mariana Trench is patient in a way only it can be.

It waits.

It sleeps.

It anticipates, and plans.

There is something sleeping at the bottom of the Mariana Trench.

It dreams of you.

Trigger Warnings

This list was compiled by the editors in collaboration with the authors. This list may not be comprehensive. If you have specific concerns, please reach out to the editors.

Without Eyes, He Stares | *blood, death, gore, murder*

A Fish-Eaten Grin | *blood, vomit, body horror, parasites*

THE REAL GENUINE HONEST-TO-GOD MERMAID | *confinement*

Boat | *blood, gore, vomit, alcohol, injury detail*

psychopompós | *death of a parent, grief, suicide*

A Night on the Andua | *body horror, violence*

Sea People | *death, violence, xenophobia of fictional creatures*

Our Yellowed Bones | *gore, implied/referenced abusive parent, murder*

Singing Sweetly Through Your Veins | *body horror, loss of bodily control*

Starfish | *gore*

Topside Topside, Do You Read Me? | *abandonment, wound detail*

From Stagnant Waters | *blood, death, ritual sacrifice, epidemic*

Endling | *animal death*

From the River the Penny Dropped | *child abuse by mother, death of a family member*

The Blood We Carry | *blood, murder, dismemberment, violence, emotional abuse*

Pastorale | *murder, vomit, blood, gore, animal death, brief references to racism*

Sealskins, Daughters, Teeth | *death of child, abandonment, domestic violence, murder*

Daughter of the Sea | *death, pregnancy / childbirth description*

Itself | *human sacrifice, animal sacrifice, sexism, ageism*

Naiad | *none noted*

Cirrata | *death of a parent, blood, gore, grief*

Everything you Dump Here Ends Up in the Ocean | *death, murder, body horror*

There is Something Sleeping In The Mariana Trench; It Dreams of You | *stalking*

The Authors

Ryan C. Bradley (he/him) has published work in The Missouri Review, The Rumpus, Dark Moon Digest, Tales to Terrify, and other venues. His first book, Saint's Blood, was published by St. Rooster's Books in April 2022. He co-hosts the Horror Hangover podcast with Cass Clarke. Learn more about him at ryancbradley.com.

Gabrielle Bleu writes science fiction and fantasy. When not writing, she watches birds and admires lichens. Their work has appeared in Archive of the Odd, Hexagon, and the Gargantua anthology by Air and Nothingness Press. Find more of Bleu's work at gabriellebleu.com.

Morgan MacVaugh (she/her) is a conductor of magic. She's recently finished up her master's in Scotland, and is now being held hostage by the last draft of her young adult novel in the foothills of Pennsylvania. You can find some of her other work in Hunger Mountain, the Sierra Nevada Review, and Luna Station Quarterly, among others.

Heath Mensher (he/him) is an award winning short filmmaker, playwright, writer, and poet. He has written for various publications and television, most notably two seasons working on NBC's "The West Wing," and has worked behind the scenes on over 40 films with directors such as Francis Ford Coppola, Spike Lee, Aaron Sorkin, and

The Authors

Paul Reiser. His fiction writing focuses on imagist horror, and he has recent publications in *Crow Calls V* and *Anterior Skies Vol. I*. He has an upcoming book of horror poetry, Glances Through Waxed Paper, and is currently working on a full-length novel, *RIPT*. Heath writes original horror flash poetry daily on Instagram as: @heathmensherauthor.

Samantha Ryan (she/her) is a writer from Tulsa, OK. She earned her degree in English Literature and Creative Writing from the University of Tulsa where she was the recipient of the S.E. Hinton Endowed Scholarship for Creative Writing. She has a chunky German Shepherd named Harley, an incredibly needy cat named Baxter, and half a dozen plants she can barely keep alive. Find her on Instagram - @samryanreally and samryanreally.com.

Michael Conrad (he/him) has been writing for fifteen years. He feels compelled to include an element of romance in all of his work, loves a good redemption arc, and is a Michigan native.

Katherine Traylor (she/her) is a US-born writer currently based in Prague. Her writing is often fairy-tale-inspired with a strong focus on transformation. She shares a home with her beautiful partner and three four-footed children. Follow her on Twitter (@amongthegoblins) or at her website, katherinetraylor.com.

C. C. Rayne is a writer, actor, and musician based on the East Coast. A lover of all things weird and discontented, C.C.'s work blends the magical with the mundane, and the silly with the strange. You can read more of C.C's stories in such places as *Bowery Gothic, Crow & Cross Keys, Grim & Gilded, Wyldblood Press,* and *Sublunary Review.* C. C. 's poetry can be found in *The Dread Machine, Soft Star Magazine, Eye to the Telescope,* and *Word West Revue.*

Tiffany Michelle Brown (she/her) is a California-based writer who once had a conversation with a ghost over a pumpkin beer. She is the author of *How Lovely To Be a Woman: Stories and Poems* and cohost of the Horror in the Margins podcast. Her fiction and poetry has been featured in publications by Black Spot Books, Dread Stone Press, Death Knell Press, Hungry Shadow Press, and the NoSleep Podcast. Tiffany lives near the beach with her husband Bryan, their pup Zen, and their combined collections of books, board games, and general geekery.

Billie Karras (he/him) grew up in the dusty Arizona desert with an ever-putrefying love of all things blood and guts and slime and sharp, rotten teeth. He spends his nights writing, his days dreaming about the sea, and is truly a romantic at heart. That heart just happens to be green. Flyblown. And teeming with their squirmy little worm-babies. You can find Billie on Instagram via @billiekarras_author.

Amy E. Casey is the author of the dark, fabulist novel *The Sturgeon's Heart* (2022). Her short fiction and poetry have been published in *Lit Angels, Marrow Magazine, Fauxmoir, Club Plum, Psaltery & Lyre, Split Rock Review,* and elsewhere. She lives and works along the cold freshwater shore of Lake Michigan, where she is writing her next book. Follow her process on Instagram @amy_e_casey

By day, **Kathryn Reilly** (she/her) helps students investigate words' power; by night, she resurrects goddesses and ghosts, spinning new speculative tales. Enjoy poetry in *Shadow Atlas, A Flight of Dragons, Last Girls Club, Willow Tree Swing, Paris Morning* and fiction in *Tree and Stone, Seaside Gothic, Diet Milk, Blink Ink,* and *Apologue of the Immortals*. Her rescue mutts, Savvie and Roxy Razzamatazz, hear all the stories first. When she's not writing, she's rewilding her suburban backyard. Twitter: @Katecanwrite

Samir Sirk Morató is a scientist, artist, and flesh heap. They are a 2022 Brave New Weird shortlister and a F(r)iction Fall 2022 Flash Fiction finalist. Some of their published and forthcoming work can be found in Rejection Letters, Seize the Press, and Neon Hemlock. They are on Twitter and Instagram @spicycloaca.

KT Wagner (she/her) writes speculative fiction surrounded by gnomes, gargoyles, and poisonous plants, in the garden of her home on the west coast of Canada. She enjoys daydreaming and is a collector of strange plants, weird trivia, and obscure tomes. KT's short stories are published in magazines and anthologies. www.northernlightsgothic.com and @KT_Wagner

Annemarie Bennett (she/her) is a Texas-based horror and sci-fi author who boasts a creative writing degree. She has published poetry and flash fiction and has placed first in two fiction writing competitions. She also placed third in a statewide Arkansas poetry competition. In her spare time she enjoys staring at her bearded dragon and thinking about ghosts.

Cormack Baldwin (he/him) and **EV Smith** (he/she/they) are partners in multiple senses, crime included. Cormack used to help with fish cannibalism studies run out of an abandoned lighthouse, and EV used to spend their spare time in the morgue. Now they work together to run Archive of the Odd, a speculative found fiction magazine. You can find Cormack at cmbaldwin.carrd.co or @cormackbaldwin on Twitter, and you can find EV at @icelandicrain on Twitter.

Malda Marlys (ey/em) teaches science just outside Chicago and writes the sort of speculative fiction that requires too many qualifiers for the normal flow of conversation. Fortunately the SFFH umbrella is wide (and kind of spooky and full of brass fittings and snakes). An out-of-practice black belt, mediocre birdwatcher, and terrible knitter, ey spends most of eir time being bullied by disreputable housepets and adding to a monumental TBR pile.

Hope Elizabeth Kidd is in the MFA program at the City College of New York. She lives in Harlem with her husband, her five children, and an assortment of pets in an 800-square foot apartment. On a typical day, you can find her drinking mochas, complaining about laundry, shuttling kids, or listening to an audio book. For non-fiction, Hope enjoys writing about motherhood, mental health, and body image, and she is writing a memoir about her childhood in Zimbabwe. She has been published in MUTHA magazine, and this is her first fiction publication.

Jan M. Flynn's (she/her) short fiction has won international Writer's Digest awards, appears in *The Toronto Journal, Far Side Review, Bullshit Lit, Midnight Circus, The Binnacle, Grim & Gilded,* and *Noyo River Review* as well as anthologies. Her essays appear in *HuffPost Personal,* and in multiple publications on Medium.com. She is the producer and host of a weekly podcast, "Here's A Thought" for people who overthink. She lives in Boise, Idaho with her husband and a cat who is charming but not to be trusted. She's represented by Helen Zimmermann Literary Agency, New York.

Victoria Nations (she/her) writes Gothic and weird horror, often about creatures with emotional baggage. Her fiction appears in *IN SOMNIO: A Collection of Modern Gothic Horror, Blood & Bone: An Anthology of Body Horror by Women & Non-Binary Writers,* and *Dangerous Waters: Deadly Women of the Sea,* among other publications. Her poetry appears in Magpie Messenger Literary Magazine, *HWA Poetry Showcase,* Volume IX, and the Bram Stoker Award-nominated anthology, *MOTHER: Tales of Love and Terror.*

K. F. Hartless (she/her) is a free-spirited fiction writer and word trapeze artist. When she's not juggling her career as a literacy specialist, she's preparing her latest death-defying act on the keys. Recently, she's been published in *365tomorrows, Luna Station Quarterly,* and *Last Girl's Club.* Check out her *Yard Sale of Thoughts* at khartless.com for fresh finds.

Anemone Moss (she/her) grew up in the forests of the Sierra Nevada foothills in northern California and now lives in the outskirts of the SF Bay Area where she writes speculative fiction.

Bridget D. Brave (any/all) hails from the dead center of the USA. A lawyer by day, Bridget spends her remaining waking hours writing weird horror and playtesting tabletop RPGs with the Wandering Monster Cast. Find more writing and weird anywhere online at beedeebrave, especially at beedeebrave.com.

The Editors

Jes McCutchen (she/her) is a neurodiverse writer of queer YA science fiction and fantasy novels where basically everyone gets a happy ending. She has two novels: *Chronicles of My Alien Invasion Life* and *A Mean Piece of Water*. When she's not writing or editing, she works at a community arts center, encouraging creativity in the next generation of weirdos.

Victoria Moore (she/her) is one of the owners of Whitty Books, an independent bookstore in Tulsa, OK. She said that 2023 was the year she would stop taking on new projects, and then promptly co-founded both a printmaking studio and a publishing company. She spends most of her days picking up things that the cat has knocked onto the floor and asking her Google Home what human foods are safe for dogs to eat.

H. V. Patterson (she/her) writes horror poetry and fiction. You can find her work in anthologies from *Black Spot Books, Shacklebound Books, Creature Publishing, Flame Tree Press,* and *Eerie River*. She also runs Dreadfulesque, promoting women in horror. Tell her spooky facts on Instagram @hvpattersonwriter and on Twitter @ScaryShelley

Acknowledgements

First, thank you to all the writers who submitted and trusted us with your work. We are constantly overwhelmed by the number of you out there who believed in this project and trusted us to pull it off.

Second, thank you from the bottom of the lake to all of our Kickstarter backers who made this project possible. Your support kept us afloat, and allowed this book to make it into the world.

Brian Bohanon, Bridget D. Brave, Brutus, David Swisher, Deborah Owens, Dison Puntillo, Dr. Andy K, Edward Maher, Gloria Hole, Haley O'Brien, Holly Wall & Ed Sharrer, Jayne Bear, Jean C. Bacon Dix, Jennifer Dix Brown & Robb Brown, John Ellis, Julia Gulia, Kye Handy, Leah Weyand, Loki DeWitt, Melanie B., Meredith Haas, Mindy Gudmundson, Nicholas Johnson, Pam McCutchen, Pam Vrooman, Rebecca Rowland, Maenad Press, Rhys Owens, Richard & Mary Perisho, Rilen Anstett, Rob Murphy, Sean Horkheimer, Tammy & Rilen Anstett, Tina Wall & Brian Peters, Tyler Thrasher, Zach Fountain, Zack Fissel.

Thank you to Kendall Whittier Main Street for offering grants and funding opportunities that helped us establish Horns and Rattles Press and got us off to a solid start.

Victoria: Thank you to Jes and Helen, for being the absolutely perfect crew to make this dream a reality; I've

Acknowledgements

had such a blast working with the two of you. Thank you to Julian, for just like... everything– I can't concisely state all the ways you have helped me grow. Thank you to my mom for teaching me to love books and words, and for thinking so highly of me even in moments when I don't. And last but certainly not least, thank you to everyone that believed in this project and trusted us– we owe all of you a great debt.

 H.V.: Thank you to all my family and friends. I'm so fortunate to be surrounded by such supportive and lovely people. Shoutout to Whitty Writers for being the best writing group! Thank you to Victoria and Jes. I would be absolutely lost without you. Big thanks to my Mom, my first reader and biggest supporter of my writing endeavors. You've made me a better writer, editor, and person. And to my husband: thank you for your unwavering support and encouragement in writing and in life. Your kind, goofy, loving presence shines brightly enough to illuminate the deepest, darkest depths of the ocean.

 Jes: Thank you to Marshall for going along with just about every whim I have. I love you. And to G who might be too little to know how much literature means to me, but hopefully will someday understand why mom is locked in the bathroom writing again. To the little weirdos I get to teach and who remind me daily that art and science are part of the same world and combined with curiosity, everything is better. Also to Victoria and H.V. The two of you are so immensely talented and creative and I can't imagine doing this with anyone else.